CW01632852

HOPES AND DREAMS

Teenage lives

Part 1

"Life is a journey that must be travelled no matter how bad the roads and the accommodation" – Oliver Goldsmith

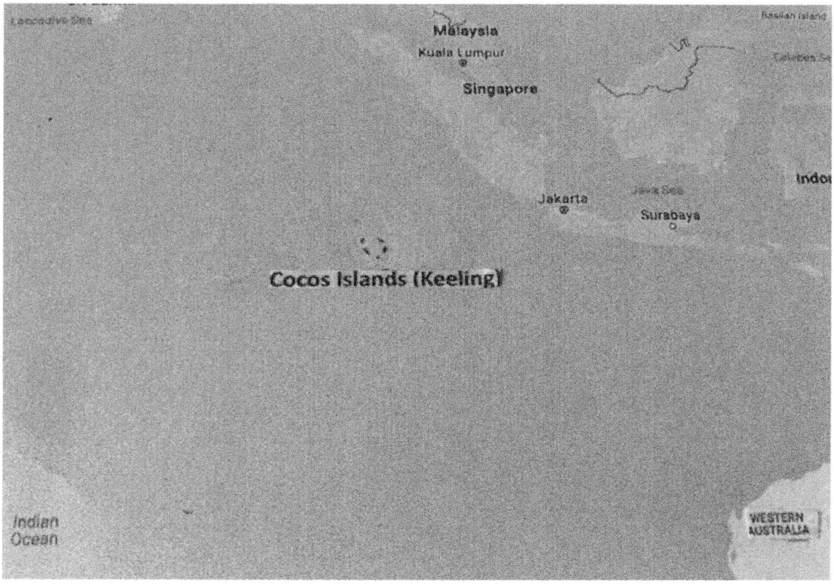

These are the Cocos Islands in the middle of the Indian Ocean
where Kaleem lives with his family.

Their closest neighbours are Malaysia and Indonesia to the East,
India to the North and Australia to the South West.

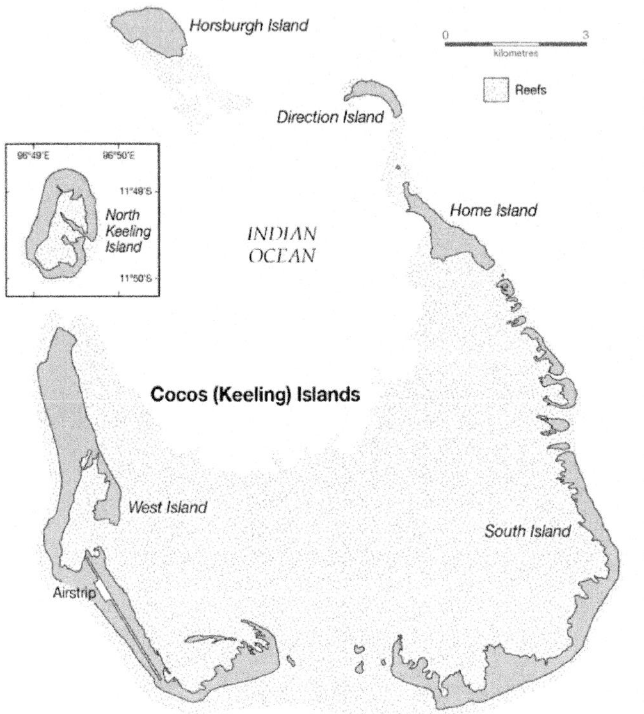

The 27 Cocos Islands
Home Island is where Kaleem lives

Chapter one

Kaleem

Deep into the Indian Ocean, surrounded by turquoise sea, lie two coral horseshoe atolls comprising 27 tiny islands with white-sand beaches, palm trees and lagoons lulled by warm south-east trading winds.
West Island is fast becoming a popular tourist destination especially for Australians as these Cocos Islands fall under the control of their government. Across the lagoon, lies Home Island, where generations of Malay Muslims have made their home. A supply boat arrives at the jetty every six weeks to provide those items that they cannot make or grow for themselves. There is now an airport on West Island that brings tourists, the more intrepid of whom prefer to board the boat and motor across the lagoon to Home with its fewer amenities and simple charm.

The Malay people were brought to these islands by a Scottish trader in the early 19th century to harvest the copra (the dried sections of the flesh of coconuts that provide oil). Eventually the Europeans took residence on West Island making it more commercial, leaving the descendants of those early Sunni Muslims to create their own peaceful community on Home Island.

Kaleem lived with his parents and grandfather, Nek Su, on the South-East corner of Home Island where, years ago, Nek Su had built a small shack from wood in a tiny clearing surrounded by dense palm trees. Its location and its corrugated tin roof helped to protect it from the worst ravages of the cyclones that hit the island from time to time. It was a beautiful spot, surrounded by gentle breezes, calm seas and an uncomplicated life. Not many people lived near here as it was a long walk to the other side of the island where others preferred to build their homes along the little "street" within the shadow of the cyclone shelter, close to the small market kiosks, the little Pula Cocos museum, the island school and the newly-built mosque. Nek Su was now finding the walk difficult and tiring but Kaleem always accompanied his grandfather and helped him along the way.

Omar, Kaleem's father, loved this quiet place where he could live and work in peaceful harmony, at one with his natural and familiar surroundings. So too did the rest of this tightly-knit family. Kaleem's mother had lived in the main Street before she had married and she had met her husband when she served on her father's fruit stall. She would ask Omar about his home on the other side of the island. When he took her there, she fell in love with it and with him. Kaleem was born there a few years later and when his Amma Grandmother had died, they helped Nek Su to bury her close by.

Omar had his small rowing boat on the nearby beach and every morning at dawn, he would go through the trees and row out into the deeper waters of the bay where the colourful fish swam alongside harmless sharks, giant rays and sea turtles. Some days, it could be several hours before he had enough of a catch to return and walk the two miles along the sandy path to the centre of the village near the jetty where he might exchange his fish for a chicken and some fresh vegetables. Growing was not easy in the sandy soil.

Kaleem went out on the boat with his father sometimes and he loved to trail his fingers through the cool, clear water. He would dive from the boat and collect shellfish. He liked to feel them in his hands, their smooth hard shells all different shapes and sizes. He liked the wide ones like grooved fans and the curve of the ones that rolled round into themselves. He loved these little creatures and happily returned them back into the waters unharmed.

The family lived a simple life in their one room home, all sleeping on mats on the sandy floor. Most of their meals were prepared outdoors under a flimsy shelter where they gathered for supper to share the events of their day and offer their thoughts to each other. In the early evening, when the daily tasks were done, the family would sit together until the light faded. Kaleem loved this special time with his family. His mother taught him how to make palm baskets. Her hands were nimble and skilled and she and Kaleem often laughed at Kaleem's clumsy attempts. With her patient help, he soon began to make passable baskets of his own. His father would sit quietly, often repairing nets and Kaleem would spend time watching and learning in anticipation that one day this would be his responsibility and he would be the fisherman who supported the family. He respected his father and knew that he was loved. Nek Su aroused Kaleem with stories about the history of the islands and the buildings that he had helped to erect. Kaleem sat cross-legged and listened in awe to the hard life that his grandfather had endured. Nek Su inspired him by his courage and determination.

None of them had left the island but they had all attended the little school where big maps and pictures had made their eyes open wide with amazement. They had heard stories of earthquakes, volcanoes and gigantic waves which were exciting but none of them had ever travelled to other islands. Of course, they knew first hand about cyclones and had endured occasions in the past when they had been forced to move into the island cyclone shelter until the danger had passed and they could return to whatever remained of their shack and the surrounding trees. The family would drag Omar's boat the long walk to the Street where the shadow of the buildings offered better protection. When he was little, Kaleem used to ride in the boat along the sandy track but now he was fourteen, his strengthening muscles were needed to help the family. When you have few possessions, it is not difficult to rebuild your home and your life with a shared love.

Kaleem's mother Aisha worked on the small plantation where she would pick and pack bananas. It was a backbreaking job. Many creatures lived among the bushes and trees but most were harmless. After work, she would go to the market kiosks and fill her palm basket with oil, spices and local flour to make samosas and flat bread. She would prepare their supper in the wok, adding fish or chicken with some vegetables, if her husband's day on the boat had been rich in harvest. Nek Su was now too old to work but he collected nearby wood and sticks, tending the fire and looking after simple repairs to their home.

Kaleem's young legs had no trouble walking the distance to the little school every day where he was taught numbers and English. Like his father and grandfather before him, he loved looking at the maps and was amazed at how tiny their island appeared in this vast ocean. He learnt the names of the continents and wondered what other boys' lives were like. His dream was that he might travel to Mecca one day. He wasn't very good at maths but he tried hard so the teacher was pleased with him. He always enjoyed listening to stories and then painting big pictures full of tall mountains and forests of trees. Living in his remote area and being mostly with adults, Kaleem found it difficult to forge relationships with the other children. They were friendly enough and sometimes he might join in a game of football in the dusty area outside the school but for the most part he was a serious child, preferring his own company. This allowed him to develop his own thinking and learn about himself and life. Sometimes he was teased but his innocent face soon made his friendly tormentors realise that they should leave him alone. Secretly, they wished that they could have such a contemplative disposition. It was a sort of quiet envy that is normal in children.

On Wednesdays, the pupils were taken to the mosque for their religious learning. Many of them saw this as a duty rather than a pleasure. They covered their heads with Kufis before embarking on the short walk. Kaleem leapt along the path. His heart stirred when he saw the shining dome through the trees. The mosque had six wide steps that circled around the front, leading to two large open doorways. The building was timber framed and the walls were painted bright white. The low roof was designed in four triangles leading up to a dome shaped minaret painted in the island's flag colours of green and gold. The children who wore shoes left them abandoned haphazardly on the steps. Kaleem slipped out of his simple slippers and rushed up two at a time in his bare feet entering the cool, dark vestibule with its cold stone floor, to be greeted by many of the old men who waited quietly for this youthful weekly invasion.

This was Kaleem's favourite day when he could be inside the glory of the mosque and feel close to god, learning the wisdom of the prophet Muhammad. He was excited to discover that one of his wives was called Aishah, like his mother. Sadly, his name wasn't on the list of his children but one of the wise old Imam's told him that they were all his children. At first this confused Kaleem as he already had a father but as he began to understand the concept of God, he knew what it meant.

The children walked reverently past the men's main prayer area with its candles burning, to the wooden balcony at the back that was the area reserved for the women and children. Kaleem couldn't wait to become of an age where he could kneel and pray with the men on the red mats in the centre of the mosque. He looked around at the white walls with their intricately carved wooden decoration and at the low ceiling with its mystical reflection of shimmering candlelight. Once all settled, a magical hush descended. The children were handed paper sheets with passages from the Quran, the holy book, and the old men would direct them to pronounce the sounds and words, while explaining their meaning. By the end of the session, the children were expected to try and chant the passage all together. Most of them found this a bit tricky but persevered out of respect for their teachers and their families. Kaleem tried his best and although he made mistakes he loved the sound of the chanting around him.

After the lesson, sheet of words clutched in their hands, the children were offered sweet biscuits and fruit juice in the vestibule that they were allowed to take outside so they could sit on the steps and relax. They returned their cups inside, retrieved their shoes and careered back to the school room to release their pent up energy.

In the afternoon, they would spend time copying the words from their sheet, trying to remember what they said. The teachers in the mosque had told them that it was more important to be able to recite them by heart than understand what they meant as Allah would understand but Kaleem wanted to know.

At the end of the day, he couldn't wait to run home from school, call out to his grandfather that he was home then weave his way through the dense layer of palm trees where he could sit on the shore. There before him the white sand stretched out and the sea was a shimmering sheet of turquoise reaching to the horizon. He loved to sit comparing the majesty of the mosque with the overpowering strength and beauty of nature. The trees whispered a promised peace as the soft waves rippled gently in and out.

Running his hands over the ridges of coloured shells that had once housed some of God's tiniest creatures, he was enthralled and enriched. Everything came together here; the giant and the miniscule, the vibrant and the passive, the strong and the vulnerable – all so different, so perfect in their own way, yet all needing each other to create their intricate, mystical pattern of life – a world to which Kaleem knew he belonged. One day as he leant back against the knobbed trunk of a palm tree, he said to himself, one day when I'm old, God will take me in his embracing love and I will understand it all.

Kaleem fell into a deep, peaceful sleep.

He dreamed he was in the blue waters swimming with the fish. He lay on the back of a large black ray whose strong flapping wings took him for a gentle undulating ride while a shoal of little fish, all brightly patterned in beautiful colours, formed an escort around them. As the ray swam from under him, it was replaced by Nek Su who was lying on his back and smiling at Kaleem, holding him steady with his strong, gnarled hands. He too let him free and Kaleem dived down into the deep water. On the sandy floor, he could see the outline of the many rocks but they were smooth and round and gold. He touched them, then stroked them with both hands and they appeared to shine more, creating a magical light all around him.

When Kaleem surfaced, he could see his father's boat in the distance. It was upturned and he thought he could make out his father floating nearby. As he swam towards him, he seemed to move further away so, frustratingly, Kaleem could never get close. The more effort he made with his strokes, the more the waves were disturbing the water forming little mountains, their white foam beginning to shower him. He turned back towards the shore to return to the shallower water where he could see his mother waving at him. Now as he swam towards her, instead of pushing through the water, the sea seemed to be moving with him as if he was being pulled in a strong tide. The water took him through the palm trees and past his mother.

“Kaleem. Kaleem.”

He woke up suddenly to hear his mother’s voice calling from their hut. It must be supper time already, he thought so he jumped up from the beach and ran in his bare feet through the trees.

The family talk over supper was focused on the festival of Ramadan which began the next day. Now was the time for muslims to fast in daylight hours. It was to help them to have compassion for the hungry. Also, it allowed them more time from their daily duties to study their holy book, the Quran, to grow in spirituality and to be forgiven by their god, Allah, for any past wrongdoing.
This would mean the family getting up before sunrise to eat their breakfast of bread and fruit, fasting and at the end of the day, waiting for their long-awaited supper until sunset.

The giving of gifts was a problem for this generally poor community on Home Island so they chose to exchange food with their neighbours and give a tiny donation to the running of the mosque. Donations of rice and other fruits and seeds were an acceptable alternative for those who had no money. Kaleem had been weaving some small mats from palm leaves to give to his friends at school.
In richer countries, new clothes are worn for Ramadan but here on this tiny island, Aisha had bought simple

white cloth to make a new head covering for herself and white kufis for the men, including Kaleem. Although the Eid ul-Fitr festival marking the end of Ramadan was celebrated by some families together in the street near the jetty, most outlying families like Omar's preferred to return home and celebrate with their family by lighting candles and experiencing a peaceful meditation.

Kaleem was hungry throughout the days of Ramadan although he never complained. He understood the spiritual purpose of this fasting even when his tummy ached for supper.
On the morning of Eid ul-Fitr, the family began their journey to the mosque shortly after sunrise. Everyone from the island would be there and he was very excited. The early morning had a coolness that made their walking easier. They moved slowly to accommodate Nek Su, whose old bare feet touched the ground tentatively with each footstep. He used a stick with one hand while putting his other arm around Kaleem's shoulders. Omar and Aisha carried baskets woven from palm leaves and laden with the food that they would offer to their neighbours.

As they neared the village, Kaleem looked out for a first glimpse of the gold and green dome of the mosque glinting through the trees and with every step, more of its white walls were revealed. Others were gathering on the path too as this small throng of worshippers came to together, heading for their spiritual home where they would meet each other in the presence of Allah.

Kaleem climbed the wide, shallow steps of the mosque, removing his woven shoes, confident of finding them again among the many pairs being abandoned there by the respectful worshippers. Entering through one of the tall arched doorways, he trembled at the mystical silence, but he was quickly pushed along in the throng of women and children moving towards their raised wooden balcony at the back. From here, he could see the mass of kneeling men below moving like a white sea, through gentle waves of humming prayer.

He slipped on to one of the wooden benches at the front of the balcony and looked across to the minbar as the elderly preacher climbed carefully up the tiny, curved steps, clutching his robes with one gnarled hand and holding heavily on to the slim wooden rail with the other. The men sat up now with crossed legs and waited. This was a special day of preaching, and Kaleem prepared himself to settle and listen to the old man's lengthy sermon. He didn't fully understand all that the old man shared, but he could see from his posture and the way he spoke with such quiet conviction that he had great knowledge to impart. Kaleem always concentrated thoughtfully, yearning to learn more of the mysteries of God by merely being part of this spiritual community.

He glanced towards the other platform where the reader was already reciting verses from the Koran. Soon this part of the worship would end and he could turn his whole attention back to the preacher. Such was the expectant atmosphere of the mosque, Kaleem knew God's presence was here, surrounding him, and a deep love burned inside his heart. He wanted to shout out with joy but his duty as a young boy was to listen and wait. One day, he might be on that platform reading or even standing there in the minbar sharing *his* wisdom with others.

Leaving the mosque and retrieving his shoes, he leant quietly against the bark of a tree in the shade.. Kaleem waited while his parents exchanged their goods. He wanted to be alone with his thoughts. He was also impatient to return home as today, Ramadan had ended and they could have a simple feast as soon as they returned.

The journey back was long, hot and tiring. His breakfast fruit had been consumed hours ago. Alongside his mother and father, his feet moved mechanically in time with Nek Su's through the sandy grass, encased by tall bushes. His thoughts were that God was with him; listening and watching, guiding and inspiring. He knew too that Nek Su needed him and that he wouldn't let him down but he was desperate to shed his responsibilities and run to his favourite place on the shore.

As they neared home, Kaleem slipped off alone towards a clearing beyond the trees. There before him the pale sand stretched out towards the ripples of the shallow sea that reflected the sun. Nothing stirred in the heat of the day. The small white crabs had dug into the sand for shelter and the fish had swum further out where they could ride out the heat in the deeper, cooler waters. Even the colourful insects and sea birds seemed to be respecting the silence.

Kaleem ran his fingers through the warm soft grains of sand and smiled. Nothing could spoil this feeling of contentment. All his needs were met and he wanted nothing more. He sat still and listened. There were no sounds apart from his mother's gentle tapping of the wok through the trees. Wafts of delicious frying food came filtering through so Kaleem knew they would soon be having their special feast. This was the one day his father didn't fish so they would all be together to enjoy this celebration.

Kaleem heard a gentle rumbling in the distance and looking towards his father's little white boat resting a little way along the shore. He could see it rocking gently for a moment or two. He felt the sand shiver beneath him. It wasn't the first time that he'd noticed this. Sometimes, it happened on very hot, still days. He'd even mentioned it to the friends at school. They'd laughed and called him "crazy Kaleem" as they did whenever they were caught and embarrassed by his need to express sensitive thoughts. They never stood still enough on the beach to notice any such thing. His mother had told him the vibrations were an echoing caused by God showing his disapproval in some other land far away. His grandfather had told him stories of mighty earthquakes which made buildings collapse and volcanoes erupting hot liquid which engulfed everything nearby. This was mostly beyond Kaleem's understanding.

He knew he couldn't sit for too long as he had to help his mother with preparing the meal. He brushed the sand from his scant clothes and began to walk back through the tall trees, closer towards the enticing aromas from the wok. As he walked, he could hear his father's voice quietly talking to Nek Su and helping him to sit on his special seat under the shelter.

Checking there was no help needed, he sat on the mat at his grandfather's feet and they feasted on crab, coconut rice and bread with the hot vegetable samosas that his mother had so caringly prepared. They ate in companionable silence, each involved in their own thoughts. When they had cleared away, Nek Su began one of his rambling stories of aeroplanes and crowded places. Kaleem thought then that he would love to take his family to Mecca.

After a while, Nek Su and Omar fell into a well-deserved sleep while his mother sat happily plaiting a new mat. Kaleem slipped through the trees, returning to his special place to swim in the shallows and reach through the crystal water to collect shells to add to the collection. He took off his top, waded in and dived smoothly into the gentle ripples. The water seemed cool so he didn't stay in long. Walking back to his special spot next to the tall tree, he sat down in the sun thinking about the inner joy he felt being part of God's beautiful world.

Occasionally, he thought he could hear a faint, distant rumble. He recalled his grandfather's story about the time long ago when the bottom of the ocean far out to sea had quaked and the seas had risen, towering above the horizon like a tall mighty wall and other islands far away in their ocean had disappeared under the water. It was rumoured that many people had drowned.

Kaleem's attention was caught by a little wave on the shore which, instead of bubbling gently towards the beach, was being sucked back slowly, with no new one trickling in to take its place. He sat up looking curiously, waiting for the new wave to creep in but the water kept receding and he could hear it drawing the little pebbles and shells with it. He listened for the insects in the trees but all the creatures were silent as if they had left and gone in search of another paradise. Something had changed. He listened again and gazed up and across the still waters to the hazy horizon until his eyes became scorched by the brightness.

The ground shook a little, ruffling the sand. Then it shook again a little more violently and tiny rivers of sand slipped into narrow gaps that were opening around him. Kaleem jumped to his feet as the cracks were deepening and the grains were cascading into them like waterfalls. He looked around and began running back towards the shelter of the trees.

Behind him, silently, on the horizon a gigantic wall of water was building.
The rumbling had intensified. Frightened for his family, Kaleem ducked and dived through the trees as the ground started splitting beneath his feet. Now these firm strong trees wavered uncertainly towards him as their roots were uplifted. He came within sight of his home where he could see his mother standing, pan in hand, staring beyond him towards the sea. She had a puzzled expression of horror and pain on her face, one that he'd never seen before.

He stopped. He turned to look behind as the last human sound he heard was his mother's low scream, "Kaleem" before an enormous dark shadow surged, wrapping him in its cold embrace and lifting him on his way, tossing his slight body against tree after tree as its watery strength shattered him and engulfed all that he had known.

Afghanistan
JK
HP
Pakistan
PB
UK
Nepal
UP
RJ
Delhi
BR
GJ
India
WB
OR
MH
TS
KA
AP
Bay of B
Arabian Sea
TN
KL

This is India. Delhi is where Aadhira lives

This is a glimpse of life on the railway lines in Delhi.

Rural farmers can't make a living from their crops
because of a lack of water due to reduced monsoons.
Also waste products from new industries are polluting the rivers.
Many families are forced to migrate to big cities like Delhi
but they struggle to find work and somewhere to li

Chapter two

AADHIRA

The capital city of India is Delhi. It is split into two halves; the area of Old Delhi which houses its history where its narrow bustling roads are overcrowded with market stalls, food sellers and poor homes. The streets are chaotic with precious cows wandering free, dead dogs lying on the road, homeless begging people and young boys pulling rickshaws for wealthy tourists who want to experience the "real" India. New Delhi, on the other hand, is an ever-expanding town of tall glass buildings, exquisite luxury hotels and a magnet for new businesses of all kinds. The avenues are wide and surrounded by pleasant green spaces.

The underbelly of the city of Delhi is her slums.
Aadhira lay on her back and gazed up at the moon – a moon full of promise and hope as her name suggested. Its luminous glow shone through the gaps in the torn mosquito netting that her father had rescued from a scrapheap near the station in New Delhi. It was some small protection against the ceaseless drone of the mosquitos and flies that hovered around on these hot July nights. The air was still and oppressive, laden with mixed smells of sewage and decaying vegetables. Again tonight, her father was out searching for any materials that would

help to stabilise their tin and cardboard dwelling. His labouring work had all but dried up and the future looked uncertain. He'd taken her older brother Arun with him to try the new hotel building sites in the city in the hope of finding some discarded offcuts which they could use to use as a cover for the roof. Their last one had been blown on to the railway track that ran within touching distance of this endless row of shanties and had been crushed beneath the wheels of one of the trains that passed by at high speed. It was commonplace here in this slum for people to suffer the same fate. Aadhira's mother had died on the tracks a few months' ago.

Aadhira lay silent and still so that no one knew she was there alone in their ramshackle shelter even though she could hear the rats sniffing around trying to break into anything they thought they could find. Most of her thirteen years, she'd lived beside the creatures that scavenge around the slums, but she didn't want to be bitten. Last time, her sores took a long time to heal and she hadn't walked well for weeks. Now, with her mother gone and her father busy trying to feed the family, she knew that she would have to do more for herself and the family, which meant not getting sick or having any trouble.

She was comfortable enough lying here on her bed of old clothes, with her long hair acting as a pillow, but that empty feeling of hunger never left her. The family could claim support from the NGO centre that was further down the track near the station but, despite using it sparingly, the ration of rice, maize and salt wasn't enough to last the month. Aadhira was a petite and pretty girl which worked in her favour when charming a few rupees from the tourists on the station platforms. The sight of this lovely, innocent but thin girl in her torn, dirty clothes and her big, soulful brown eyes often added fruitfully to the family purse. She had to be alert and quick in avoiding the railway officials who would chase her off. Tourists were an easy target; the level of their generosity often increased by Western guilt.

Although the slum dwellings were illegal, the local charities did what they could to help these homeless people who had nowhere else to go. Many poor families had travelled long and arduous journeys from the countryside where their land had been taken and where there were now no opportunities for work of any kind. Hundreds of large groups, turning up in big cities, had erected these make-shift homes, crushed together, back to back and on top of each other within a stones throw from the railway track. Some of the train drivers slowed down but many, fearing a backlash if they didn't stay on timetable, charged through obliterating anything in their path.

These temporary shacks were erected quickly but disintegrated just as quickly in the wind or the rains as they were built mainly from cardboard, plastic and tin, wedged by pieces of wood and held together with old string and wire. Doors and windows were flimsy old bits of material. Women and children would sift through the mountains of garbage on the other side of the track to find rags and remnants so they had some privacy. Sometimes they needed to use them to replace their worn out clothes. Aadhira's shack was one small cubed room built on top of another. She and her mother had always slept in the one above which meant she could look up at the stars and the moon at night. They had found an old wooden ladder to climb up but being on the top still didn't deter the hungry rodents.

Across the other side of the tracks near the trees were some corrugated iron toilets with high cubicles that allowed the waste to fall into a pit. They were erected by the authorities after much persuasion from the railway officials since they were not for the convenience of the dwellers but an attempt to prevent tourists having to watch the people relieving themselves openly in public. These were mostly used by the women for privacy, while the men continued to urinate anywhere and often defecated between the railway lines. So the problem still existed in part. The queue and the smell was often a strong deterrent but women and girls were vulnerable to attack if they chose to go elsewhere. Despite there being no running water in the toilets themselves, there was a water pump stationed nearby. Occasionally it gushed out generously a dirty brown water but mostly the pressure was poor and filling a vessel could be a tiresome process. Bottles, once filled, were taken back across the lines to be boiled for drinking and cooking the hard grains of rice.

Aadhira lay and thought about her mother. She had been a beautiful young woman when she had left the countryside with her husband, full of hope for a new life in the city. She must have been appalled by what she met when she arrived but Aadhira never heard her complain about the hardships they endured. She looked after her children with sensitivity, encouraging them to be brave and resourceful, supporting her husband in any way that was possible. When she was hit by the train, her father had removed her body and had taken her to a field nearby to be cremated. He wouldn't allow the children to see her. Hard though that was, Aadhira's memory could not been blemished by the sight of her broken mother.

Every day after that, Aadhira and Arun had embarked on their daily journey across the tracks alone and vulnerable. Arun told his sister he'd look after her. They gathered the old bamboo bag for collecting firewood. They'd have to walk about three kilometres further on for that. In the past, their mother had left them by the water pump to wait for her return.
They carried 5 big empty water bottles which would be very heavy on the return journey (so long as the pump was working. It didn't always). They'd learnt the times of the trains but the busy railway timetable meant it wasn't always possible to negotiate all four tracks in one go. Often, they would get across one set and then, hearing a train in the distance, would need to lie flat by the side of the rails until the train had rushed past, its wind attempting to whip their clothes from their backs and covering them with dirt and grease.

Aadhira continued looking at the night sky remembering that first time when, like now, she had laid on her back between the tracks waiting for the train to pass. Setting out, she had stepped cautiously over the rail and on to the first sleeper, looking frantically each way while her brother urged her on with his arm around her back. He had carried the bag but she would need to carry things on the way back. They had reached the middle before he shouted the warning for her to get down. Her heart beat fast as she flattened herself against the ground and waited as the sound of the train got closer and closer, louder and louder until she thought her ears would burst. A thundering wind caught her clothes and showered her with dirt as the train rushed past and off into the distance. She had felt dizzy and afraid without her mother's hand to hold so Arun helped her up and they carried on across the track. As they neared the other side, she became more confident, shrugging off her brother's support and leaping over the rails until they were safely on the verge on the other side of the four double tracks.

Without her mother by her side, Aadhira felt anxious and alone. They agreed that Arun would start collecting firewood and then come back to the pump while she joined the enormous queue waiting for the toilet which held mostly women and lots of naughty children shouting and screaming. Impatient mothers were smacking their offspring and grumbling loudly about the stench from the overused facility. Aadhira found it difficult to maintain her place as newcomers joined and pushed in front of her.

Once she reached half way, she became part of the mass of people and was propelled along within it. The smell and the heat were unbearable.

Finally Aadhira made it into the shack itself to wait her turn. Loose sewage made the floor wet and slippery so she worked hard at staying upright with the fear of slipping over and either being covered with the foul muck or being trodden on by others desperate to take her place. She retched involuntarily several times, managing not to vomit and vowed once again that next time, she would find a place in the forest further on where her brother went to collect bits of twigs and small branches for firewood. As she exited, her spirit lifted at the thought of her new scheme and how she could collect wild berries too so long as she minded the small poisonous snakes lurking in the branches.

Being so small, she had struggled to make her way back through the crowds surrounding the water pump in search of Arun. Relieved, she saw him. He hadn't yet reached the pump but he was standing with a full bag of firewood, spending his time happily chatting and laughing with his friends. It was a lucky day as the pump was gushing and it didn't take long for everyone to get their fill of this brown essential.

Once more, it was time to renegotiate the tracks; this time, laden with heavy water bottles and a basket of wood. The basket was strong, plaited by their mother from bamboo. Arun gave his sister a heavy bottle for each hand and he balanced the other three on top of the wood, clutching the basket underneath rather than by the handles. They had edged through the crowds on the verge, many of whom were waiting to cross at the same time as them. To a chorus of "now," they jumped the first rail, then the second, ran to the next and jumped both of those before they heard the clunking of an approaching local train. Flattening themselves quickly, they had lain and waited for the train to pass. This local train seemed to take an eternity to chug by. At least its passing was less frenetic as they lay still and watched the wheels turning as if in slow motion.

Progressing steadily over the remainder of the rails, they had arrived at their shack unscathed.

Arun had helped his sister up the rickety ladder with their stores and he had gone off to find his friends again.

Aadhira had laid on her bed of clothes and had sobbed quietly at the misery that was her life.

Back in the moment of this moonlit night, Aadhira heard the sound of something metal being dragged towards the shack. Several times, it met large stones which it scraped and squealed across. She sat up and listened, recognising her father's voice issuing instructions to her brother. She peered out from the top of the shack to see her father and brother negotiating a large piece of corrugated tin between the railway line and the fronts of the dwellings. Her brother climbed the ladder as her father passed the large square tin up to him. With his strong fifteen year old muscles, he pulled it over the top, creating a sturdy waterproof roof.

The room went dark and Aadhira could no longer see the moon. Her consolation was future protection from the rain and the cold winds of the coming winter.

Next morning, the slum came alive early as the sun rose. Many dwellers had already left in the early hours to walk the long distances needed to find casual work for the day, or for a week if they were lucky. Arun went with his father leaving Aadhira to manage the daily chores of washing clothes and preparing the rice and salt. With the cover on the roof, everything was dark now so she climbed up and down the ladder several times in order to take all her jobs into the daylight. Here she squatted using the last of the cold water to soak the rice and to dunk her ragged clothes to remove some of the dirt of the last few days – at least the new roof could be used as a drying platform. When she'd wrung the clothes and place them up there, she sat on the ground, waving the flies away and listening to the emerging sounds of the day.

All around her, Aadhira recognised other girls' voices chattering and laughing in the morning sun. She used to have a few friends but since her mother died, she had not wanted to play or chat or share secrets. Somehow she felt older. Her body was changing and telling her she would soon become a woman. She was worried about the monthly bleeding and how she was going to manage. It wasn't something she could talk to her father about and the other women, her neighbours, always seemed too busy with their own children to help her or talk to her. No, she was on her own now and had to handle it.

Aadhira jumped up and decided she was going to go across the tracks on her own. She would go into the forest, collect some twigs and wild berries and fill up a couple of water bottles for when her family returned at the end of the day. Hopefully she would find a quiet spot to avoid the need of queueing for the toilets. With a surge of enthusiasm, she charged up the ladder, grabbed her mother's well-used bamboo bag and looked down the line for any trains. None could be seen or heard so she jumped nimbly over the first two rails, then the next. Listening carefully, she heard a rumble. Waiting a few seconds for it to become louder, she knew a train was on its way so she lay down beside the rail and waited. It was a slow train and as it clunked past, rather than trying to pull the clothes from her back, it disgorged showers of dirty water, soaking her by the time it had gone through. She picked herself up, looked and listened, then continued with her journey. She looked left and right and for a moment it seemed like a race as others were crossing at the same time as her. She quickened her speed as if to try and win but she didn't see some small boys in a gang coming from the other direction as they shot past her, knocking her sideways onto the sleepers. Then she heard the next train. She didn't have time to get up and jump over the rail. She'd never laid directly under a train before so her heart was in her mouth as the carriages passed overhead. The noise was much greater here and she feared for her life as it hurtled overhead. One or two had low hanging chains which brushed against her threatening to drag her along underneath. One caught the handle of her bag and started to rip it from her hand before she had time to think. She let go just in time.

When the train had passed, Aadhira lay still, her body shaking. She tried to stand up, feeling weak and shocked. She looked around her. Everyone else was walking across as usual. She was more than half way so it made sense to carry on, sadly regretting her carelessness with her mother's precious bag. She had no hope of collecting much in the way of firewood or wild berries now. What would her brother say when she told him? She would need to collect bamboo to make a new one but it was hard to pull and impossible to cut without a knife so now they had no way of carrying anything. At that moment, she realised that the empty water bottles were in the bag and they too would have been crushed. What a pointless trip this had turned out to be. She was no longer a child and she had to pull her weight, not make stupid mistakes like this.

Across on this side of the track and going up towards Delhi rather than the forest, lay a mighty garbage heap. She made her way there. It was a huge mountain about twenty metres high of mixed mess containing rotting food, household detritus, bits of rusty metal, old tyres, bits of cotton and other materials and, most importantly, discarded water bottles. Aadhira had been there a few times in the past and sat under a tree at the bottom while her mother had climbed carefully and sifted through the rubbish looking for any "treasures" that would improve their home and their lives. She remembered her mother climbing down with food and bits of waste paper clinging to her face and body with black buzzing flies circling her like bees round honey. She had a triumphant smile while holding a large piece of material in one hand and an old metal kadhai in the other. Her eyes were shining as she ran to collect her daughter, giving her a hug of happiness. Aadhira recalled the horrid smell of her mother's clothes which lasted until it was their turn to use the pump.

Now facing the colourful, jagged mountain in front of her, Aadhira realised just how hard it would be to climb. Bits of metal and glass poked out at odd angles and rotting paper made a slippery foothold. She circled the mound, looking for a suitable place from which to launch her expedition. Although it was early, it was crawling with other hunters and looked like a living and squirming hell. She found a spot and started to climb. She thought she could see the necks of some large bottles jutting out about 5 metres up. She found a footing on a metal tin. It was hot from the sun as it brushed her leg so she quickly looked for another, to move on. Every hand hold created a mass of slimy sludge in her hand that she had to shake off before she could safely move on to the next one. After a couple of metres, she gained confidence but made the mistake of looking down. Not only did that make her sick with fear, she could also feel the vomit rising in her throat from the acrid smell. She looked up again so that she could locate her destination. The whole heap seemed to be surrounded by rising steam as the heat in the air mixed with its contents. All around her people were impassively poking through the muck to get a hold on something that might be useful to take home or to sell to the vendors that waited by their stalls at the bottom.

The bottles were almost within her grasp now. As she raised her left foot to find a higher step, her leg caught on a sharp piece of metal which scored her calf along the bone from her knee to near her ankle. She cried out in pain but no one stopped to see. She carried on climbing and grabbed the top of a plastic coke bottle. She secured her feet and after much poking, prodding and pulling, she managed to extract two more of similar size. Feeling pleased with herself, she forgot about her wound, lay her cheek against some soft slime and rested, readying herself for the return journey.

Careful to avoid more damage, Aadhira climbed back down to the base. Her head was dizzy from the height and the combined smells. Covered in slimy muck, she made her way back towards the pump with her prizes. The queue was long because the pump wasn't gushing today. She planted her feet apart to give her the strength and size to prevent herself being pushed out and waited her turn. After what seemed an interminable time, it was her turn to access the reluctant pump. She half filled a bottle and used it to sluice herself down while the next was filling. When all three were once more filled, she made her way to the side of the track ready to cross.

This was going to be tricky since the bottles had no lids. She had stuffed the tops with leaves that she'd pulled from the verge but knew that some water would be lost when they, like her, lay flat for an oncoming train. The heat had congealed the blood on her wound but it caused her some pain as she lifted her leg over the rails. She made slow progress, only once having to lie down as a train passed. Slowly she limped her way back to the shack, carefully climbing the ladder with one water bottle at a time and storing them in the corner, wedging them to stop them from falling over.

Aadhira fell into a feverish sleep.

Soon she was returned to her recurring dream of the railway tracks. She saw herself sitting in the strong palm basket, each corner being lifted by four large clear plastic bottles which acted as wings. As it crossed the track, the basket flew higher and gained speed. She heard a train and tried to flatten herself down but strangely the thundering noise was beneath her as they continued to fly across. The force of the displaced air surged Aadhira up violently and precariously. She clung to the handles as she was tossed to and fro until she could feel the motion stabilising as the train careered into the distance. The trees of the forest were ahead of her now and she could smell the faint odour of the toilet shack beneath her. The wings lifted her again as they brushed the tops of the trees. The journey seemed endless as if she was lost above a deep, impenetrable forest.

She felt the basket slowing while air hissed from the bottles. She was gliding down into a clearing where fresh grass made a sea of green. Landing gently, she climbed from the basket and looked around. The tall trees of the forest had receded and in their place were soft-leaved fruit bushes of every kind. She picked a peach and bit it. The juice ran through her fingers and down her chin. It was sweet and delicious. She turned for her eyes to explore more delights. A fountain was cascading crystal spray into the rippling water in a pond. She stretched out her hand and touched it. She cupped some in her palm and drank. On the far side of the clearing she could see a small white, round pavilion, with a domed roof. The building was the size of one large room. Entranced, she moved forward and touched the walls. They were cold but pure smooth marble. Looking closely as her fingers ran over the surface, she could see tiny precious jewels of all colours – rubies, sapphires, emeralds and opals – embedded in symmetrical patterns in the marble slabs.

As she entered the doorway, Aadhira felt at peace. She had no fear as she tiptoed into a richly furnished room with red drapes and a gold chair, with its seat covered in plush red velvet. On a mahogany table in the centre of the room was a feast, a banquet such as she could never have imagined. Bubbling rich curries beside plates of soft white rice, many breads, vegetables in delicious looking sauces and batters and plates of mixed sweets – rasmalai and balushahi balls, mithai in mixed colours and slabs of kaju katli. Aadhira had never seen so much food in her small life. In a trance, she stepped towards the table. The more she moved, the further away the table seemed to become and her steps became laden and difficult. She caught her leg on something and fell over. When she turned round, it had all vanished and the tall forest trees were looming in around her. She stood up and walked towards the trees. Her basket had disappeared. The undergrowth was thick and unwieldy and she knew then that she was utterly lost and alone.

She woke up.
When Arun and her father returned late that evening, having secured a few days' work on a new building site in the city, they found Aadhira in a restless coma, her limbs flailing out as if in pain. She was feverish, shivering and still dirty. Her injured leg was covered in flies laying eggs in the wound. They carried her down the ladder and set off towards the first aid centre at the far side of the station. It was a hazardous journey as many slum dwellers were still cooking outside their shacks so her brother kept look out while her father carried her along the sleepers inside the rails on the track. Several times, he stumbled as Aadhira thrashed around. He stopped at a neighbour's shack and begged for some water to cool her head and moisten her dry lips. They didn't dare go along in front of the station platform as they would be chased away so they detoured around the back through the thick scrub and trees which slowed their progress. Alas ahead of them was only darkness which meant that the centre was closed. They found their way to some semblance of a queue and sat and waited for morning. A kind old man, walking with the aid of a stick, saw their distress and gave them a small cup of dirty water and an old cloth to try and keep Aadhira hydrated until the centre opened.

Father and son remained silent, neither wanting to acknowledge that they were terrified Aadhira might not survive until they could be seen by the health assistants in the morning. They listened to the gentle moaning of others. Night creatures scurried, murmured and fluttered in the darkness. The fear of snakes gliding close was ever present as the moon only spread a murky light through the polluted glow of the city. No trains passed but the air was filled with the regular rumble of approaching aircraft coming in to land and the hum of the relentless traffic from the city.

Morning came. The hazy sun rose. Aadhira was still and silent. Her father could hear her heart beating against his chest as he held her. People started arriving and the centre came to life. Inside its large open doorway, they could see assistants donned in pale blue uniforms with blue paper caps covering their hair and masks over their mouth and nose.
They started collecting the sick and suffering from the queue on the wooden platform outside. Blue shiny gloved hands lifted gently until the trolleys were full. It took some while for new patients to be summoned.

At last a male assistant lifted her from her father's arms and laid her on a clean trolley. He talked to her in a gentle voice while he examined her leg. She opened her eyes but there was no telling if she understood where she was or what was happening to her. He looked at her father, who had followed in, with Arun standing close up against his shoulder. He shook his head and explained that the wound was badly infected and that he would try to clean it as best he could. He gave her an injection of antibiotic and some painkiller and started to clean and dress the wound. It took a long time as it was now wriggling with maggots. He poured in cleansing fluid and eased away all the dried blood and dirt. He wrapped her calf in soft cotton bandage and told her father to bring her back the next day to have the dressing checked.

The family returned the way they had come and carefully lay Aadhira upstairs to sleep. She smiled at them both and settled into a deep sleep quickly. Her brother and father left her, hurrying back to work, hoping that the job on the building site was still theirs.

That day, a careless accident with a pan of hot oil over a wood fire spilled into one of the huts. The flames were quick to catch hold of any soft materials in their path and so they spread rapidly along the railway line. The fire snatched everything as its arms flicked to and fro grabbing what it could to quench its hunger.

Aadhira didn't stir although her senses acknowledged the smoke and the heat before her frail body was engulfed by its raging grasp.

The Outer Hebrides are a collection of over 50 islands
that lie off the west coast of Scotland.
They are sometimes known as the Western Isles.
Only a small number of the islands are populated.
When it's stormy, the islands are cut off
as the boats and planes are cancelled.

South Uist where Megan lives

Chapter three

MEGAN

The islands of the Outer Hebrides, known as The Western Isles, form an archipelago that sits off the coast of North West Scotland with Iceland and the Arctic to the north, America to the West and Ireland to the South. Over one hundred islands make up this chain with only fourteen inhabited. These remote islands in the North Atlantic Ocean are home mostly to crofters and artisans. Modern technology has created causeways between the central sections of land for ease of travel where once ferries were needed to connect them.

The beaches are long and deserted with grassy dunes and pale sands above which eagles fly high and seals swim in the turquoise seas. The ancient land of metamorphic rocks with its stone circles is a mix between uninhabited mountains to the east and freshwater lochs that intersperse the low-lying fertile grassy machair full of wild flowers and birds nesting. Crofters use the flat land for cattle-grazing, hay cutting and low intensity crop farming.

The beauty of this place is its wildness, sparse population and wide skies.

The wind whistled across the Benbecula causeway as it hurled and tossed every leaf and twig in its path. Spurts of water from the angry sea shot up spraying Megan as she hurried along this narrow road bridge that had been built to connect the islands. Her long red hair was flung across her face like a whip as a sudden gust ripped her hood from her head.

Benbecula, the tiny island behind her, was the hub of the Uist community, with the school, the shop, the telephone and the doctor's house, unlike South Uist, her home and where she was now headed. This seemed to many, especially those who had chosen to leave, like a barren, empty land only interrupted by smallholdings where the few remaining crofters toiled hard to keep a roof over their heads. Surrounding them were swathes of flat, machair interspersed with narrow rivulets winding their way from the sea and seeping into the heart of this land that time and memories seemed to have forgotten.

To her right, on the hill towards the sea, the Catholic church sat proudly watching over the lives of its congregation. When she was a little girl, the family would go every Sunday, wearing the best clothes and shoes they could muster and be part of the morning service. She loved singing the hymns and watching entranced by the flickering candles around the room and the sweet burning smell of the incense as the priest waved the silver ball around gently. Megan recalled the day when, wearing a white dress and a flimsy veil, she was confirmed with her parents watching over her, smiling. She received the blessing and the bread which continued weekly after that until the fateful day shortly afterwards that her father went missing. She was never taken to church again.

The cottage that Megan shared with her mother, Ailsa, was half an hour away from the tiny school room on Benbecula and was set in its own land, isolated and exposed to the whims of the elements. Tonight, Megan could see, while battling against the wind, that her journey would be slower and more arduous. Apart from the urgent moans of the gale around her, there was a silence in the rest of nature, nothing stirred, the animals were safe in their shelters for the night. She would be pleased to be home by the warm hearth with her mother as she had not been feeling well during the day, bothered by an uncomfortable grumbling in her tummy. In fact, the teacher had remarked on her paleness.

Now, as she neared the cottage, she saw the two dim lights coming from the tiny square windows that were set in the strong, grey stone. She began to make out the shape of the thatch roof with its matching chimneys at either end. Urged on by the dry and warm welcome she anticipated, she quickened her pace, through the gap in the dry-stone wall, approaching the small wooden door that sat between the windows.

Megan's mother had been standing by the window watching apprehensively for her daughter's return. Two past tragedies on such a night were uppermost in her mind – one that was so deep and personal that she suppressed it. The other, happening a few years back, was kept alive in their memory by the presence of the family gravestone in the local cemetery that she and Megan passed when they walked to the far beach in the summer.

She recalled it had been mid-January, a night just like this – a freezing and inhospitable time for the islands – with regular gales and high seas. Around half past six on that particular evening, a local mother had looked anxiously out of the window at the dark and wild night. The storm had been developing rapidly all day, gaining pace as it approached these outlying Islands. All the ferries had stopped running and most people had sought their homes and fires to ride out the torrent.
She and husband had moved back here to South Uist two years ago to a croft near his parents' home. This was the Hebridean dream to return to your island of birth and continue the family traditional crofting way of life. Their children, a boy of 7 and girl of 5, settled happily into their new remote surroundings near the shore far away from the bustle of Glasgow where they had been born.

Their Grandad had arrived to join them for tea around 4.30 and, as they listened to the storm gathering, it was agreed that he would definitely be needing to stay the night.

Winds in excess of 120mph had driven the wild Atlantic over the beach and across the strip of machair grassland that separated the shore from their home. Waves were now splashing against their front wall, some sending spume towards their roof, and the angry sea lifted and threw large pebbles indiscriminately into their garden.

It was not yet high tide so they had to decide whether to sit out the storm or make a break for it a mile and a half along the coast road to the other grandparents' house which was on higher, but more sheltered ground. The tea had been cleared away and the children were already in their warm pyjamas. In the end, the consensus was that staying put may be more risky as water threatened to flood their home, despite the sand bags. So grandparents were rung to tell them that the family would be making a quick dash by car to reach them before the height of the storm closed the window of opportunity.

Once the decision had been made, their mum efficiently gathered sou'westers, raincoats and wellies from the cupboard by the door and the family donned their weatherproofs; the children laughing excitedly about the adventure while behind their smiling chivvying, these islanders knew the dangers of ignoring the unpredictability of the sea.

More erratic and urgent crashing of waves from the shore hastened their departure.

They took both cars as any vehicle left behind in this storm could easily be rendered a write-off from a salt water soaking.

Battling against the wind, Grandad forced open the front door and dashed determinedly towards his car. It was nearer the road and, having reversed in, it would be easier for him to get started quickly. He grabbed for his door handle, wrenched it open and slumped into the driving seat as the door slammed behind him. Breathlessly, with shaking hands, he put the key in the ignition and set the wipers on double speed.

Dad too struggled against the wind as he shepherded his family to their car. Mum held both children tightly by the hand and, with Dad using all his strength to open the back door, she bundled them in, following rapidly behind, thinking they would feel more safe if she sat with them. Having secured them, Dad held on to the back of the car and fought his way round to the driver's door. As he did so, the edge of a creeping wave surged against his calves, nearly causing him to lose his footing. He held on and he too managed to get safely inside the vehicle.

They set off with Dad hugging closely the red back lights of Grandad's car in front for guidance as the mix of sea and rain splattered their windscreen.

Meanwhile, the other grandparents had decided to head towards them and meet them to guide them in but their car was met by an impassable well of water requiring them to make a swift reversal back up the one-track road to their house. They ran in and phoned their son, to warn him to stay put, but it was too late, the family had already left. All they could do now was watch and wait, their eyes peeling the road from the causeway for a sign of the two cars' headlights.

Entering the causeway that led to Benbecula, Grandad, in the first car, was fighting with the steering wheel to prevent the car from being blown chaotically from side to side as he forged on. He could barely see the edge of the narrow road. The sea had breached the low drystone wall and was gushing over, forming a layer of water on the road. He could just see his son-in-law's lights close behind as he gripped the wheel and held his foot firmly on the accelerator. A couple of hundred yards away, the lights of their destination were shining out like beacons in between the sheets of rain that were lashing his windscreen.
They were nearly there.

A sudden terrifying gust of wind whipped loudly round his car as a giant wave surged up, high over the wall and enveloped him. Its extended embrace captured the car behind and together they were lifted over the sides of the causeway and thrown into the raging sea.

Ailsa recalled the anger at the time and how subsequent engineering improvements had been made to all the causeways that joined this string of four islands to prevent another such tragedy. Tonight, she was thankful for that.

She caught a glimpse of Megan's slight figure and ran to open the door. It ripped from her hands, crashing back into the room sending a flurry of disorder to the curtains and whipping up anything light and loose that was in the room. The flames in the open fire reached out threateningly. Ailsa pulled her daughter gently inside and pushed the door closed.

"Are you all right?" she asked Megan, helping her to remove her dripping outer garments and closing the curtain on the back of the door.
"Go and get changed out of those wet things and we can have some tea."

Megan hugged her mother and quickly disappeared into her small bedroom. She was shivering uncontrollably, pleased to be putting on dry clothes. She emerged and stood in front of the warm sitting room fire.

Ailsa smiled at her lovely daughter as she brought the fresh soup, cheese, pickles and bread to the table. This child was so precious. They only had each other but that was enough now.

Despite its bleakness, Ailsa loved this place with its vast flat lands and the sounds from the shore nearby. Here she felt close to everything that was important in the world, although life had intervened and caused her much pain. It was backbreaking work tending the small flock of sheep, the handful of cattle and the little cluster of chickens but, since her husband died, she was determined to keep the croft. Life was hard; searching the rocky hillside on dark nights for a ewe bleating in distress, the endless hours of waiting for newborns and scratching a living from the produce that she grew in the large, rambling garden behind the house where the soil lacked richness; not to mention gathering the cows in from the machair! The chickens weren't much trouble and offered delicious eggs each morning. She loved the cottage with its small windows, its warm hearth that heated three rooms, a tiny kitchen and a barely adequate bathroom. She was comforted by the old fashioned furniture. Everything about the place was strong and solid giving her the feeling of security she needed. At times, she had to deal with animal deaths, even occasionally having to wring the neck of a sick chicken. She felt a moment of sadness when cattle or young sheep were herded on to the ferry to be bought at the livestock market on the mainland. She fought a hard battle to raise these animals and now they were being sent away to meet their fate. At least the money from their sale supported her and Megan for the coming months.

The winters were bleak and difficult, chapping her hands when she worked outdoors from early morning till late evening taking advantage of as much daylight as was available at this time of year. Summertime was different again. Although she didn't have many moments to stop and stare in her busy schedule, in those warmer and clearer months, she could look across the glistening, calm sea to the mainland hills in the distance with the sun adding its warm glow to the entire landscape. On days such as these, seeing the lobster boats puttering off into the distance, gave her a short sharp pang of pain and memories but she responded to the beauty of her surroundings which lifted her spirits once more. And, of course, there was Megan to love and cherish although a difficult parting was coming closer as Megan came of an age where she would need to go to the mainland to board for her schooling.

Ailsa put that thought away and remembered the night, like this one, that her husband also lost his life. That day, too, she had watched the heavy squalls arriving and could see the change in the sea which was restless and moody. The grey currents were swirling and strong waves beginning to batter the shore.

Her husband had insisted on supplementing their small income from the croft as he wanted his wife and daughter to have a few little luxuries in their bleak lives.
He had furnished Megan's room with a small carpet, bought a new oven for the kitchen and built them a small functional bathroom which meant they no longer had to use an old iron bath in front of the fire or go outside to the yard for the toilet.

To this end, he had bought a small boat, creating a passable living by collecting lobsters in pots that he could sell to the hotel and to visitors. That fateful day, with a storm heading across from the mainland, he had gone off early hoping to check his pots, some of which were far out into the channel. The forecast had warned to expect this severe weather from early evening but a sudden change in the direction of the wind had brought it closer sooner with the winds rushing and tossing through the channel causing the seas to turn rough and wild with high waves leaping and thrashing in the air like flames from a huge fire.

When Megan's dad didn't return, his wife had waited silently, holding her daughter by the hand. They had waited all that long day, gathering with others in the small sandy bay on the other side of the machair; not daring to look away from the mesmerising seas in case she missed a glimpse of his familiar figure, riding a wave in his tiny boat and returning to safety.

As darkness fell, reluctantly villagers drifted home. One friend took an uncomprehending Megan to sleep at their home for the night, but Ailsa waited hour after hour, standing in the cold and rain, hoping, until she too had to find the refuge of her silent, empty home.
Sadly, the tell-tale broken wooden pieces from his shattered boat were washed up and found along the shore over the next few days. There was never a body that could be buried in the bleak cemetery.

The pain was hard to bear but her neighbours had been kind, helping

her with the animals and the essential chores at first, making sure that she and Megan did not go without. However, after all this time, she still suffered that sharp sting of loss.
Finally, Ailsa had realised that, for Megan's sake, she must move forward with their lives. Although in the past many of her friends had gone to the mainland in search of the enticements of modern living, she had chosen to stay and share the life of her close-knit community, dependent on the elements and on the small provisions boat that came every third day, in good weather, to serve their needs. This was where she belonged, close to the land with its rich rewards under a vast sky and embraced by nature; one in being with the real world. Her belief in God had disappeared completely.

Megan had always been there by her side of course. Now at fourteen, she was able to share a lot of the tasks. The gentle uncomplaining girl had always taken pleasure in gathering the smooth brown eggs from the straw each day and feeding their small flock. Now that she was older, she had become involved in the heavier work too. She followed the sheep as her mother led them on her old quad bike towards the harbour for delivery to the special livestock boat. The cows were more unruly and difficult to husband but it was a rule of the croft that cows must be kept so caring for them and moving them across pastures had to be managed by the two women. Once money from the sale of the stock was received, if the previous season had been good, Ailsa was able to offer a small wage to a retired crofter for a few weeks, to help out. He would till the land around their cottage ready for planting and repair the sheds and outbuildings.

Tonight, as every night since their loss, they shared their meal with conversations about the day's events. Megan usually regaled her mother with the antics of the children at school.

Being the oldest, today she had spent a happy few hours helping Mrs. MacKinley, the teacher, with the little ones. The school had only five pupils, three of whom were younger than six. They adored Megan for her gentle patience whereas Andrew, the only other pupil who was Megan's junior by just a year, liked to spend his day teasing them until he was sent out to find wood for the fire in the classroom. He wasn't interested in learning. He much preferred action and felt his destiny was to take over his grandfather's small croft in the not-too-distant future. However, Megan had watched his face today as she told them all the story of Bonny Prince Charlie and his escape on a rowing boat to Skye with the help of local heroine, Flora MacDonald.

Mrs. MacKinley also taught Megan the maths and English and biology that she would need to extend her own education. She had aspirations for Megan. She wanted to encourage her to experience a wider world by taking up a boarding place in the mainland school in the next year or so. Secretly, Megan had other ideas. There was no way she was going to be parted from her mother nor from the simple life they led together. She was content and allowed herself to explore the world by reading in any of her spare time. She loved reading stories, especially historical novels, many of which, like Bonny Prince Charlie's adventures were based on embellished facts. She explored the world with atlases and picture books, comparing her farming life with those of the children in African countries whose climates were so different from her own. In fact, Mrs. MacKinley was trying to set up a penfriend for her in Kenya. Megan thought this was very exciting and looked forward to writing and to receiving interesting letters in return. Ailsa tried to show enthusiasm, knowing deep down that her daughter needed the opportunity to experience the wider world but also knowing just how much she'd miss her.

This evening, Megan was unusually quiet so Ailsa recounted an amusing anecdote about one of the chickens that had escaped from the pen and fluttered up in an ungainly flight on to the back of one of the cows where the hen promptly started scratching as if she was in the yard. The cow let out an outrageous mooing which scared the chicken who leapt off its back and landed in the water trough. Spluttering and scrabbling, it tried to get out but had failed. It would probably have drowned if Ailsa hadn't been on hand to pull it out unceremoniously by the neck and shake the water off. She put it down and, squawking indignantly, it strutted off back to the safety of its gang who tutted and muttered together.

After tea, Megan stayed resting by the fire and her mother peered out of the window as the rain continued to tap fiercely against the glass violently rattling the frames. The wind seemed to be worsening. Often, in the winter months, the high seas would mean the ferries were cancelled and the islanders would be left to find provisions from their own cupboards rather than relying on fresh supplies. Ailsa was always ready for this and kept a well-stocked larder.

Sleeping by the fire was a welcome relief for Megan as she had been feeling unwell most of the day. She didn't worry her mother that she'd been feeling a little sick with a dull ache in her stomach that had turned into a sharp sudden pain every so often. Now, falling into a deep troubled sleep, moments from her day began to manifest themselves in a strange but vivid dream (as they do) where her telling of the story of Bonny Prince Charlie's escape merged with her own biology study of the life cycle of frogs and a new exciting word "metamorphosis."

In her dream, Megan became Flora Macdonald preparing a disguise for herself and the Prince in order to escape to Skye. So the strangely matched pair, disguised in servant's attire, left the stone cottage, treading cautiously through the machair, avoiding the criss-cross network of shallow streams. The wind was cool and strong, creating its own high-pitched whistling overriding the gentle thud of Flora's laboured steps. The Prince on the other hand walked lightly on tiptoe seemingly charged with an energy of expectation.

Reaching the agreed inlet, the water deepened and opened into a wide channel leading to the sea that separated these Outer Isles from their destination, Skye. There was no sign of the boat that should have been there to transport them to safety.
Charlie cut a strange figure, tall and muscular in overflowing, white feminine attire as he paced the shoreline impatiently glaring into the distance. His hem was covered in mud and the ribbons on his lace cap were snatched by the wind, that threatened to whisk it away in an erratic dance.

Flora turned her back on the unsettling presence of Charlie and his restless striding. She gazed at the broad, open landscape before her. The light of the moon reflecting on the water created a jagged line disappearing into the far horizon beyond which lay her dreams and her future. The gusting wind smacked at her face, whipping her hair across it while the grass under her feet, made wet by the cold night air, was silently seeping into her boots and saturating the frills around the base of her long petticoats.

This was her land, her heritage and nothing could tear her from her deep sense of belonging. The smell of the sea took her back to her childhood when she would leave these shores with her father to go fishing. Occasionally, they would stray further from land and meet the stronger currents that flowed between the islands. She remembered the exhilarating thrill of the little boat being tossed around like a cork, yet confidently staying afloat in the squall. She was never scared, always feeling safe and secure in the embracing presence of her strong father. She welcomed the wind rushing through her hair then and the sudden showers of spray spitting against her face.

Now in these less certain circumstances, Flora opened her eyes. Still no boat in sight.
Succumbing to a sudden physical exhaustion and drained by the mixture of negative emotions that she had been struggling with since meeting her surly companion, Flora slumped quietly down onto the ground, lying flat out with her back resting on the wet grass. She stretched, reaching out her arms backwards along the ground past her head, yielding to the moment. She linked her hands loosely but, devoid of any control, they locked together in an iron clasp and she found she was unable to release them as her arms had stiffened. She couldn't move her elbows and her wrists had become taut and unbending. From this position, she formed the curved shaped prow of a boat. In panic, as she tried to sit up, her rounded spine locked into a keel and her torn petticoats wrapped the exterior like a coating of white paint. At the same time, her heavy straightened legs, feeling ever more wooden and stiff from the walk, seemed to detach from the rest of her body. With muscles tightening, her knees refused to give and her lower limbs transformed into a pair of strong, wooden oars attached to the oarlocks.

Terrifyingly, Flora's long red plait had dried out transforming into a robust mooring rope which, at that very moment, was grabbed by strong hands that were pulling her towards the sea. Taken by surprise, and feeling the rough grass scratching at her back, she was launched into the water where suddenly she felt calm and free, exhilarated by the sensation of floating, bobbing around with the cold waves lapping against her. She was overwhelmed by a new energy, ready for what lay ahead.

She was strong, confident that she wouldn't capsize even as the heavy weight of Charlie stepped in. He was unaware of this transformation as indeed he seemed unaware of anything that didn't directly affect his own mission. In his haste to be away, without a backward glance to locate the whereabouts of his missing companion, or indeed any thought of how the boat had magically appeared, he grasped the oars and pulled her out firmly into the channel.

Megan woke with a start as her mother was gently shaking her shoulders. The dream, or nightmare really, had distressed her. Tears formed and ran down her pale face.

"What's wrong?" her mother asked, worried sick.

Megan looked up at her mother.

"I was having a terrible dream. It was a stormy night and I was helping Bonny Prince Charlie to escape to Skye and my body became locked into the shape of a rowing boat and he used me to cross the sea."

"Goodness," said Ailsa, "but you're here now in the safe and warm. If the weather deteriorates, the school will be closed tomorrow and you can stay here and help me."

At that moment, another sharp pain shot through Megan's body, making her jerk and registering the pain on her face.

"What is it?" her mother asked, concerned.

"I've had this pain all day and felt sick and now it's getting worse."

Ailsa went to the medicine cabinet, collected a glass of water and encouraged Megan to take two pain killers.

"These will work soon. It's probably best if you go to bed. You'll feel better in the morning."

She helped Megan up from the chair by the fire and led her across the room to her bedroom. The girl was almost bent double. Her legs were wobbly and her face was white.
Once she had settled, Ailsa looked out again at the increasing storm as she closed all the curtains.

Megan slept fitfully for a couple of hours but once again a surge of pain made her cry out. This time the pain hadn't evaporated; it had remained severe. As Megan was such an uncomplaining girl, her mother knew this was serious and that she would have to venture out in the storm to collect the doctor from Benbecula. His home was further down the road from the school room so it would be a difficult journey for her. The quad bike was out of action so she had no alternative but to run.

“I’m fetching the doctor,” she told Megan, who smiled weakly and lay her head back on the pillow.
“I’ll be as quick as I can.”
Ailsa was used to going out in bad weather to tend to the animals so her waterproof clothes were ready by the door and she was able to put them on quickly. She pushed the curtain aside but the pressure of the wind made the door difficult to open. Once she’d managed to she created a small gap, she was just able to pull it enough to slip out before it slammed again behind her.

She rushed headlong into the pelting rain, the howling wind whipping at her clothes as she ran into the darkness. The path was slippery and dangerous now and several times she nearly lost her footing. Struggling to stay upright, she reached the causeway. The waves were crashing angrily against it as she made her way across this exposed stretch. The wind pulled her this way and that. She had to hold on to the barrier to stop herself from being blown away. Nearing Benbecula, she could see a few lights from the scattering of houses. She made her way past the school room and the shop, eventually having the doctor’s house in her sights. She arrived exhausted at his door.

Without a thought for the conditions outside, the doctor took little time to grab his coat and his bag, bustling Ailsa into his car and driving her back the way she had come. The rain lashed the windscreen and the squalls pushed the little car this way and that. Arriving at their cottage and getting out of the car with some difficulty, he followed Megan's mother up the path and into the house.

Megan was still lying prostate on the bed in obvious pain, her face white and her body shivering. Shedding his coat, the doctor knelt calmly on the floor, by her side.

"Where is the pain, Megan?" he asked.

She pointed to the place where it hurt the most and he gently probed her abdomen with his strong, confident hands, searching for an answer. She attempted to smile bravely at him until she took a sharp intake of breath when he found the nucleus of the pain.
He knew at once. It was appendicitis. He turned to Ailsa.

"We will need to get Megan to the hospital on the mainland," he said quietly. He looked steadily at her.

"I'll just pop back to the village and call through to the mainland on the radio to send the helicopter." He left the cottage and they heard his car disappearing into the darkness.

While they waited for his return, mother and daughter sat together holding hands both with hearts pounding as they listened to the thrashing sea and howling wind.

Now back in his house, with a sense of urgency, the doctor removed his outer clothes and sat down at his desk. After fiddling endlessly with the controls of his radio transmitter, he finally established a connection.

“I’m almost certain that the patient has appendicitis,” he told the hospital. “She needs treatment urgently. We need the helicopter to collect her.”

Deep down, he knew that nothing could take to the air in weather such as this so he was not surprised when the reply came that they would see what they could do and get back to him.

He returned along the treacherous route to Megan’s bedside, to give her some stronger pain relief and reassurances that all would be well. Megan smiled gently while her mother exchanged worrying glances with the doctor who was attempting to look positive and optimistic. Once the medicine had given her some small relief, he took his leave and braved the journey back to sit by his radio transmitter. It remained silent.

Several hours elapsed and Megan’s condition worsened. By this time, she had fallen into that world of pain that excludes all else. Her mother felt helpless.

In the early hours of the morning, however, came the news over the radio that the wind had lessened and the helicopter was taking off. It would be with them in just over half an hour and the hospital was ready and prepared to receive Megan for immediate surgery.

A weary but relieved doctor struggled up the family's path for the third time that night to prepare his patient for her airlift. As Megan's mother lifted the latch, the pain that he saw in her face told him that it was too late.

Two weeks later, a small, sad and broken procession of all the members of the community, wound its way to the little cemetery overlooking the sea once more and Megan was laid to rest close to the family who had lost their lives in that other unrelenting storm years before.

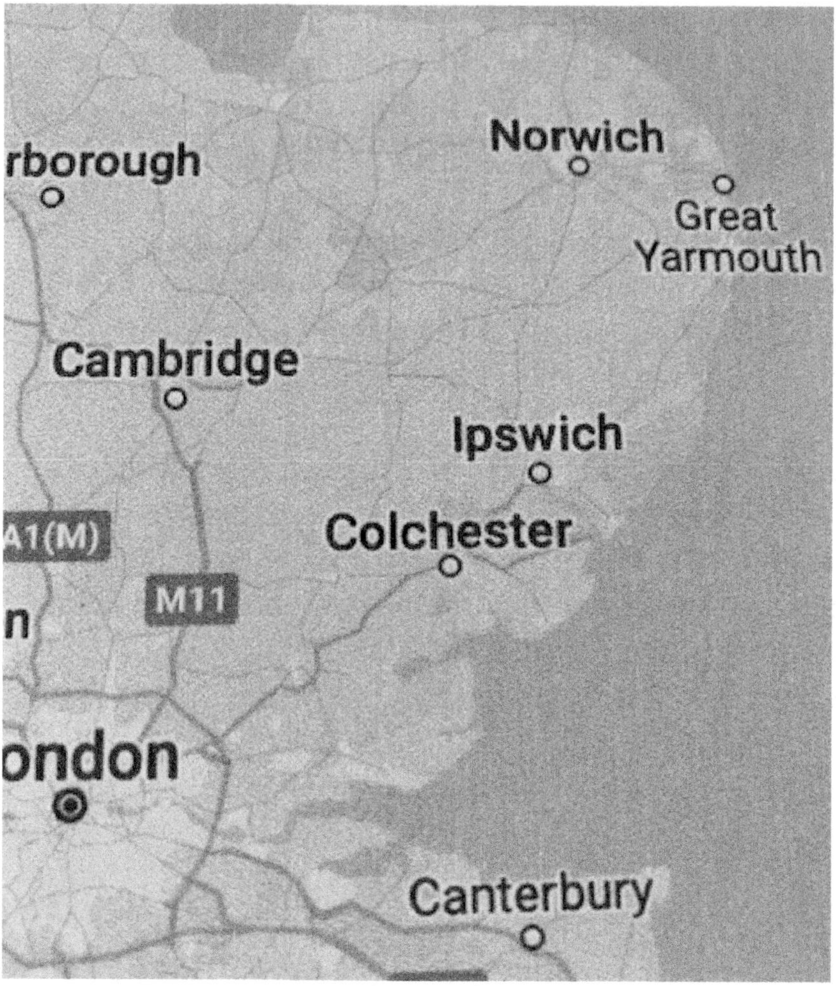

Great Yarmouth is a large seaside town

on the East coast of England

Great Yarmouth is very popular in the summer
with loads of holidaymakers but, in the winter,
when most of the amenities and amusements close down,
it's very quiet.

Chapter four

MARK

Mark lived with his parents on the outskirts of Great Yarmouth, a large seaside town which is said by many, especially returning holidaymakers from the Midlands, London and Essex, to be a fun, lively place. In summer its promenades are bustling with holidaymakers whereas in the winter, it's deserted and quiet apart from the gulls. Locals to the town are loyal to its charms whereas those in nearby villages (such as Mark's family) tend to avoid the summer crush and use the town for a quick fix of silly fun, a cheap beach supper of fish and chips or winter walks on the long promenade that accompanies the miles of sand from Gorleston in the south to Caister in the north.

The open, vast main beach is great for bouncy castles and buckets and spades but a dip in the cold North Sea is only for the exceptionally hardy or a very hot summer. The wide concrete prom is comfortable for pensioners, pushchairs and little pedal bikes.
Further along, where the gentle dunes shelter nesting skylarks, it's a perfect place for a quiet winter walk. In the summer months, the skylarks' distinctive song directs you to look high above to see them hovering protectively over

their nests. If you're lucky you can watch their sudden vertical drop down on to the sand.

Gorleston Beach to the south is more up-market with its meticulous landscaped three-tiered promenade. Large expensive houses flank the coastline where the views are wide and wonderful. It's food for the soul to sit on one of the many dedicated wooden seats and gaze out towards the horizon watching the occasional comings and goings of the pilot boat as it welcomes a large cargo ship into the port. Even in winter, on a sunny day, the sea sparkles with its reflection, like little white Christmas lights.

Mark's family could only have afforded a small house in Gorleston, so they chose to buy a big one on the northern outskirts of the town where they are much cheaper as new builds are constantly being squeezed into the spaces available. They lived in a quiet cul-de-sac near to the bypass, a short drive from the beach. They had lots of holidays abroad so they didn't feel the need to pay for a sea view.

Despite Mark being the only child, the family chose a 5-bedroom executive home so that Mark could have two rooms; for an uninterrupted night's sleep in one, thus avoiding all the blue lights emanating from the mass of technology he had packed into the other. Unbeknown to his parents, however, like a lot of teenagers, he spent half the night in his games room anyway while they slept peacefully unaware, in the belief that they were perfect parents.

Mark's mother, Debbie enjoyed all the luxuries that life could offer. She had had a simple and secure upbringing with her father working as a bus driver in Basildon and her mum staying at home to look after the house and Debbie. Anything that Debbie wanted, she was able to have either because her parents had the money and saw the need or because she was able to wheedle it out of her dad who was wrapped round her little finger. She left school at 16 and went to work in an office. Very soon, she became quite independent, spending her money on nice clothes and evenings out. It was on one of those evenings, at the local favourite night spot, she met Mark's dad. Their relationship developed with great speed. They had a joint interest in buying whatever their money could buy and they were married when she was just 18.

Mark's dad was from a large family where he and his siblings battled for space, time, food and money. He resolved firmly to leave home, get a well-paid job and have his own home as soon as possible. Their first married home was a small terraced house in nearby South Benfleet from where Mark's dad could do the daily commute into London to work as a car salesman in an upmarket BMW showroom. The perks on the side were good and they had a comfortable life financially especially as, before Mark was born, his mother worked full time too. As a car salesman, his job was a moveable feast and before long, they decided to move to Norfolk which they felt was a less frenetic and potentially dangerous environment to bring up Mark. So they chose the outskirts of Great Yarmouth. He set up his own car sales business on the outskirts of Norwich while she stayed at home giving Mark the attention they felt he deserved.

The family led a superficial life, totally absorbed in their own affairs and wellbeing. They went to Spain on the Costa Brava for their annual holiday and had money to spare to have weekends away in nice rural retreats in the UK. They dined out frequently and employed a cleaner and a gardener for a few hours a week. Life was rich and they knew few boundaries in pleasure and self-indulgence. They rarely saw Mark's grandparents although they phoned regularly once a week. Mark had to be promised a treat to get him to talk to them for more than a couple of minutes.

As a holidaymaker in Great Yarmouth, If you have money to spare, Marine Parade offers endless rows of slot machine arcades that cash in on the frivolous spenders' misplaced optimism. Crammed in between, are the gift shops that sell cheap souvenirs; everything from t-shirts proudly displaying, "I love Great Yarmouth," beach paraphernalia and naughty postcards with rude pictures of fat women with thin husbands. Scores of cafes, restaurants and food kiosks offer customers a good, cheap meal with no frills and fuss. Attractions, large and small, line the wide pavements from the funfairs at either end with much entertainment in between.

Mark, now thirteen, was excited about the prospect of freedom to explore the excitements of the town. His main interest was the arcades where he thought his wiliness could make him some money. He had been promised a new mountain bike for his birthday as the walk was too far from his home and the buses were too intermittent. Mark had tried the bus once but was frustrated by all the old folk who took too long getting on and off at every stop. On return, he had called his mum to come and collect him.

Two piers stand proudly out into the sea. Entering Wellington Pier, there's a sense of déjà vu as its dull interior holds yet more fruit machines, although it does host a bowling alley.
It is fast becoming a refuge for the asylum seekers housed in the local hotel who have nothing to do but wait.
Approaching Britannia Pier, the wide entrance entices you in for fresh doughnuts, fish and chips and sticks of rock. There's a live seaside summer show, more cafes, bars, open-air bingo, a fun park for all ages and that special chance to look through the cracks as you walk, to see the sea below. Mark, like all kids, got down on his hands and knees to stare at the waves. He'd been given a smart phone (too young, of course!) and had nearly lost it as it slipped from his pocket, landing perilously close to one such gap.

Mark's family had moved here from Essex a few years ago. His Dad ran the car business which kept him busy several evenings a week and at the weekends, although

some days he worked from home. Now Mark was thirteen, his mum had taken a part-time job in a local village garden centre, making lunches in the popular café. She was a chatty lady and made lots of passing acquaintances Mark attended the local high school, a short distance away.
He was, by default, a materialistic boy and, having no siblings, he was able to wangle most of what he wanted from his parents. His constant nagging had been for the bike. His father had told him that his new car, a BMW X5 was first on the list, together with more furniture and furnishings. His mother took every opportunity to take trips to Norwich for a "better quality" of purchase.
Mark had been promised the bike would be his before the start of the summer holidays.

The changes in the seasons on the stark East coast can be delightful for those who are akin to nature. In Autumn, the sea becomes wilder with crashing waves and the wind whips up the spray leaving lumps of scummy foam balls rolling along the beach. Warm sunny days can unexpectedly appear giving the chance for a walk along the shore to see what shells may have been washed up the previous night. Turnstones have the same idea as they run this way and that in groups on their fragile red legs, poking their sharp little beaks along the line of the turning tide to see what they can uncover. Occasionally a pair of wagtails may be seen bobbing up and down nosily and leaping around on the sand. Seals patrol the shallows looking for places to give birth.

On colder days, last year's new gulls begin to feel the chill under their wings and, floating majestically, they glide high above the sand with the backdrop of a leaden sky, still and calm but eyes alert for the promise of titbits. Their wiser counterparts begin their forays into the inland landscape in search of food along the rivers and the ploughed fields.
Daily arrivals of geese and swans from colder northern climes, like countless Red Arrow formations, reach the coast, loudly gabbling, heading for sheltered spots in and around the fields where they can rest out the winter.

Mark rarely noticed the changes in the seasons, or anything related to nature. For him, Autumn meant going back to the confines of the classroom and the daily battle with his mother about not wearing his coat or jumper. Why couldn't she understand he didn't feel the cold? When the pupils were allowed out on the grass field at playtime, he would catch those late summer daddy-long-legs offering squealing girls the choice of "hold it in your hand or I'll put it down your neck!"

Through into winter, things pick up a bit with ice and snow high jinks and the opportunity to create a bit of mischief. School had banned snowball fights but Mark had found a way to cause cold and wet distress, especially to the younger pupils by surreptitiously putting snow in their hoods as they emerged into the playground.

Snow is beautiful in the fields as it settles and glistens in the sun. Schools in the villages close and children can enjoy the delights of the mountains of drifting snow that build up on the roads. In the towns though, the buses continue to run so routes are cleared by gritting lorries giving town children no excuse to stay away. They plod their way laboriously through the mucky slush until a big overnight freeze creates dangerously exciting slide runs in the ice. As you can imagine, Mark loved these, extending them wherever possible, regardless of the pensioners who might need to get to the shops. On such days, when Mark finally arrived home, he'd shake himself off in the hallway, shedding his wet and often muddy clothes along the hall floor before leaping barefoot up the stairs to the safety of his games room, shouting over his shoulder to his mother to bring him a frothy hot chocolate and cake. Mark's family didn't venture out on cold, wet or windy days unless it was essential. They had home deliveries from Waitrose and Amazon and Mark's dad often worked from home, leaving his staff to sell his cars.

The seasons moved on with Mark solely focused on early summer and getting his new bike.
Crocuses peeping through the cold soil are one of the first signs of spring, followed by the marsh marigolds on the edges of ponds, yellow dancing daffodils, creeping aconites and bushes of broom. This welcome invasion of yellow was enough to warm the heart as new life emerges from the depths of winter and brings hope to many people who have struggled through the cold, lonely and dark months. Mark made his own enjoyment by picking bunches of free daffodils to impress his mum on Mothers' Day and stealing birds' eggs, either to smash for fun or to

add to his hidden collection. He knew he shouldn't but couldn't see why?

Mark expected life to be one long round of fun, but it was often interspersed with irritating punishments for his behaviour in school. This only happened when he didn't manage to wriggle out of the blame. For example, one morning, Mark had been late for school as was often the case. He hadn't hurried because it didn't matter to him. In his school bag, was the detention letter that he'd decided not to give his parents. He ambled cockily into the classroom after the register had been taken. The teacher ducked out of a confrontation with Mark so early in the day.

At break time, he had gone into a shaded corner of the playground to dole out the daily ration of sweets to the younger pupils who hovered around him. Mostly these innocents were unaware of the contract they were entering when agreeing to be his friend. Not many of his peers approached him since they had often been victims of his volatile and unpleasant nature. No one split on him for fear of repercussions.

After lunch, Mark had been called to the head teacher's office regarding the letter that was still lurking in his bag. Smirking irritatingly, Mark lied that he'd forgotten to give the letter to his parents.

“This is just not good enough, Mark!” Mr. Crabtree, retorted angrily, staring at the smug expression in front of him.

“I can’t help it if I forgot, sir,” Mark replied feigning innocence.

Mr. Crabtree knew of old that this discussion would not end well for either of them so he informed Mark that his parents would be asked to come in for a meeting; not that Mr. Crabtree was optimistic for a satisfactory outcome to that either.

“Is that all?” Mark asked.

Mr. Crabtree shook his head.

“Mark,” he sighed, “you are a bright boy. Why don’t you use your cleverness to improve your attitude? There’s no end to what you could achieve with your ability.”

“Thanks, Sir,” replied Mark. “Can I go now? I’m missing my football lesson.”

The interview ended as many did with Mark’s behaviour not set to improve and
Mr. Crabtree wondering what else he could do to instil some discipline into this wayward, spoilt boy whose parents did not support the school’s authority.
Mark laughed to himself as he put on his football boots. Stupid old fool, he thought. I can do what I want.

At the end of the day, Mark meandered slowly home from school, calling in at the newsagents to replenish his sweet supplies. What he produced at the counter was a small percentage of what he had secreted into his pockets in a dark corner of the shop. Pleased by his little fraud, he sauntered cockily along towards his road, hood up and looking down to ensure he didn't meet the eye of any of his passing neighbours.

"Hi Mum," he called as he came through the back door.

As he entered the kitchen, his mother confronted him bravely.

"The school phoned, Mark," she said as he commenced his raid on the fridge.

"They want to have a meeting. Something about a missing letter that they gave you to give to us?"

"I don't know anything about a letter," Mark lied. "You know that secretary at school; she's hopeless. She probably got it all wrong!"

"Anyway," said his mother, "apparently, we have to go to discuss your recent behaviour."

"I haven't done anything Mum. They're always picking on the likes of me because they're too scared to tackle the

bullies whose dads would come down to the school and thump the teacher."
"Well," said his Mum, "I'm sure it's a mistake. Your dad can go down and straighten things out with the Head. After all, he did give that big donation to pay for all the football team kit. They should be grateful!"

Mark smiled again. It was so easy to manipulate people. When he was older and running his own business, he'd have a fine time treating people like puppets and organising their lives for his profit.

Later that night, after spending several hours on his play station, Mark was unusually tired and went to bed. He seldom called out goodnight.

However, this night was not a happy one for Mark. He had a vivid dream.

He was pushing the button on the side of his gaming chair which catapulted him into his television screen. He found himself driving a fast silver convertible sports car that seemed out of control. His hands were on the steering wheel but the car was driving itself. What's more, his feet couldn't reach the brakes. The bodies of dead deer were lying randomly on the road as it rushed towards him. His car swerved this way and that trying to avoid them – all at great speed – and with minimal success. Cloven hoofed legs flew up into the air and squashed bloodied bits of flesh hit his face before the road entered a forest.

The car slowed down to walking pace. For a moment, Mark thought he might be able to jump out, but the seat belt was trapping him in and he could find no way of clicking it open. In his lap there were dozens of birds' eggs of different patterns and sizes. So, he sat there frustrated and a little bit frightened. Clamorous chattering and muttering were coming from the branches overhead and, as he looked up, he saw flocks of shiny, black rooks with menacing claws, bobbing their heads up and down as if in a conversation that was getting more and more heated.

Then, with one accord, the rooks took off with a tremendous flapping of wings. They surged in a squawking, frantic mass towards him. Some tried pecking at his head and face. Others rested on his arms and on the car. Mark pushed them away but they kept coming back at him. The rest of the flock flew alongside, in front and behind, surrounded him like an armed guard.

The car stopped and the rooks all lurched on to the road where little bikes were waiting. They peddled away into the heart of the forest. Now Mark could see the tall trees again. He was confused to see their trunks morphing into the infants from his school, all marching towards him. They were silent. Their eyes staring. They moved steadily closer, balancing their mighty foliage above them. He looked up and saw the leaves were beginning to fall from the trees, leaving skeletal branches. He was mesmerised. He forgot all about the stationary car as the leaves became bags of brightly coloured sweets – smarties, liquorice of all shapes and sizes, sugar lollies on sticks, toffees in gold wrappers, M & Ms and hundreds more. Meanwhile, the children's arms had been released from the trunks wherein they began to pelt Mark with little cream filled Easter eggs which split open on impact, revealing their white and yellow slimy centres.

Bracing himself with his forearms against this onslaught, Mark realised the car was moving again. It had whooshed out of the forest, leaving the sticky mess behind. He could see he was approaching a straight open road that stretched on and on towards the horizon. Flat desert sands spread out on either side. The only life to be seen were random cacti that stood on the spot, moving their fat spiky arms up and down like robot sentries.
The car sped on, the wheels dislodging all the sand until Mark was enveloped by an opaque cloud. He shielded his face but the sand found its way into every crevice, flying up his nose, rushing into his mouth , scoring his eyes and filling his hair.

Mark screamed "I need water" at the top of his voice and he sat up suddenly to find he was in his bed, listening to his mother's footsteps rushing up the stairs.

"What's the matter?" she asked breathlessly.

Mark looked confused, tried to recall the nightmare but it was fading fast.

"You must have had a bad dream," his mother supposed. "I'll get you a drink of water and you can settle back down again."
Mark took some while to settle, disturbed by the horrendous experience, finally falling back into a troubled sleep. His mother didn't wake him in the morning. She let him rest and have the day off school.

Early in June on a Friday afternoon, Mark wandered in from school to find his father unexpectedly at home. Both parents smiling smugly at him as they ushered him into the lounge, and there, centre stage, was his brand new mountain bike.
A Carrera Vengeance, top of the range, black, adjustable forks, 16 gears and double-walled rims on the wheels. His heart gave a lurch as he rushed up to check it out.
He turned to his parents,

"Thanks Dad. Thanks Mum. It's fantastic! Can I go out on it now?"

Dad shouted "yes" emphatically while behind mum's smile lurked a little niggle of worry about safety.

"You will be careful, won't you?" she asked.

"Of course," he replied as he shot upstairs dumped his school bag, changed his clothes, grabbed some money and bounded back down the stairs two at a time.

Without further ado, he wheeled the bike out through the front door and was off, his parents watching him proudly from the window.

Summer is, as we know, a noisy and vibrant time in the heart of Great Yarmouth and Mark sped into town to indulge his dreams – slot machines, chips, doughnuts and generally having a great time. Today the world was his "oyster." The Caister Road to the main town has a wide pavement and cycle path running parallel. This gave Mark the opportunity to try out the multiple gears and get used to the bike while not having to worry about the cars speeding along the bypass. Gaining confidence, Mark tried to race them while almost knocking down a man and his dog.

By the time he'd negotiated his way through the traffic to Marine Parade, his legs were feeling a bit wobbly and tired so he queued for some chips to take out. Smothering them in salt and vinegar, he wheeled his bike to the promenade and sat with his legs dangling on the beach wall. Many of the holiday makers had already left the beach to go home for their dinner, so Mark sat and watched the seagulls hovering hungrily over his bag of chips, then landing and waddling towards him until he flicked them away. On the beach, the donkey rides had finished, so too had the boat trips to Scroby Sands.

Doughnuts were next on Mark's list so he jumped up and cycled along the pavement till he came to the kiosk where he bought a bag of five for £1. He took them back to the

prom riding handsfree while he stuffed all these sugary delights into his mouth.
Now for the arcades!

He propped his bike up against the Silver Slipper entrance and headed for the change kiosk at the back. He had about £5 left so changed it into smaller denominations to give him a chance to sample all the machines. At first, he had a winning streak, excitedly rushing from one machine to another, waiting for the sound of the dropping coins pumping out into the tray before scooping them out. He even had success on the "crane" where he lifted a cheap watch. He hit the jackpot on several machines and managed to roll in some coins to push the pennies off the shelf and win some sweets.
He was having a great time until he realised that he was dipping into his pockets more and more and no longer winning.

Feeling a bit let down by the world, Mark looked out towards the road. Having run out of money and noticing that it was getting dark, he decided it was time to leave. His bike! He'd forgotten all about his bike. He was buoyed at the thought of riding it home. He hurried through the machines arriving at the point where he'd left it. It wasn't there? Frantically, he looked around and then he saw that a couple of young lads were leading it away on the other side of the road.

"Hey!" he shouted. "Stop!" as, without thinking, he ran across the double lanes of traffic.

At that moment in time, all the young driver in his silver convertible saw as he screamed along was a flash of clothing. He never got to his brakes. He hit Mark at 60 mph and there was nothing anyone could do except watch in horror.
Mark was crushed and broken like an errant roe deer.

Speeding on
Along a soft tunnel
Of gentle colours.
Like human arrows
They race towards
A promised land.
Passing over
Ancient walls
And golden temples.
Lands of red roofs
And snowy slopes.
Golden prairies
And shimmering deserts.
Green fields
And fast flowing streams,
Craggy mountains
And wide oceans.
Higher and higher
Into the milky depths
Of the magical stars
And beyond
Towards a new home
A new beginning
Where hope heralds
A soft landing.

Kaleem, Aadhira, Megan and Mark travel beyond the Earth.

They will meet beyond our world.

PART 2

Hope smiles from the threshold of the year to come, whispering 'it will be happier'..." – Alfred Lord Tennyson

Kaleem was the first to arrive.

Opening his eyes slowly, he gazed at his surroundings. He seemed to be in a vast room with no defined edges, where the walls and ceiling receded into a distant haze. There was no colour, just a creamy-white atmosphere with reflections coming from a richly glowing large opening further down the room on the left-hand side. He could see no furniture or furnishings. The floor was soft yet solid against his bare feet.

He was near the back of a long queue leading to that bright glow. Around the vast areas of the room, others were standing, alone, in their own special space. Everyone, including him, was dressed in white robes. He looked down at his feet and held out his hands. He was surprised to see that he appeared unscathed – no broken bones, no lacerations, not even a scratch? His body looked as perfect as that of a new-born baby.

The room was light and although it was full of people, there was a strange emptiness – perhaps it's because there's no embellishments or boundaries either, he thought. No one was moving or interacting – an atmosphere of peaceful silence prevailed. Those standing in the centre of the room didn't have an expectance of joining the queue in which he found himself waiting. There was merely a sense of patient acceptance.

Kaleem looked around and tried to think about where he might be? The ambience in the room reminded him of the mosque. Not that it had the same exquisite beauty and colour but the tall walls and high ceiling gave him that same feeling of a powerful yet gentle embrace. He had always had a spiritual awareness and now here he could feel the presence of God. The large opening like a huge, rounded archway, towards which his queue seemed to be edging had a powerful bright yellow glow emanated from within it, drawing him in even though he was way down the line. He surveyed the space again to see if there was anything earthly with which he could associate but there was nothing recognisable and he realised that he must be in another place away from the earthly world that he'd known.

His mind cast back to his island home and his family. He recalled the tsunami and the rush of warm water that engulfed him and tossed him about like a toy. He remembered seeing a tall palm tree right ahead in the path of the wave that carried him and the sharp thud as he hit it at high speed. He wondered where his broken body had ended up and now he realised it was still here, intact. He thought about his mother whose scream pierced his soul as he passed her by in his watery canopy. She too would have been caught up in the wave and his father and grandfather too. None could have survived this onslaught. Perhaps the entire island - the school, the mosque, the cyclone shelter, the street, his home - all might now be for ever under the sea? Now, none of it seemed to matter. All these earthly attachments were irrelevant. He was near to God. He could feel his presence.

Kaleem felt a small movement and looked more closely at those in the queue. Before him was a line of many people, some looking around, some with heads bent slightly, all facing the same direction. Very few turned or moved or spoke; mostly they were old. There was a woman holding a sleeping baby and a man hand in hand with a small child who was gazing around in slight confusion. He found himself slightly closer to the dazzling light and adjusted his position so that he could try and work out what happened at the front. He was still some way off but, in the distance, he could see that there was a figure, standing to the side, looking rather like one of the teachers at the mosque who always waited to welcome everyone in. Some people passed through without any interaction with him. Sometimes one who had reached the front of the queue would lean across to talk to man whereupon they would receive a nod or a quiet response. Occasionally this doorkeeper would touch the person gently on the shoulder and say a few words. After the brief exchange, those people would move out of the line and drift into the central area, some seeming to be lost from sight. Those he could see, stopped in a space and stood still.

Kaleem was overcome with a sense of peace. He felt no urge to look back on his old world. He was so overcome by this feeling that he knew there was no need to look elsewhere. He knew that God had been with him all his life and this was the climax of his spiritual being. No longer did he need to listen to the old man in the minbar. Nor would he need to become a man and be among the group who sat cross-legged on the wide, open floor of the mosque. He was free from earthly connections. The distant whisper of the trees and the waves on the shore now seemed to have been nothing more than a fleeting moment in time; his family and experiences but a vehicle in which he had travelled.

Kaleem turned to look behind him. Several more had joined the queue now. Next to him was a small Asian girl, who had a child-like expression of surprise. She smiled tentatively at him.

"Were you caught in the tsunami too?" he asked her.

She looked puzzled and shook her head.

"No. I was lying asleep on my bed when the fire came. I could sense the smell of burning and the heat of the flames licking at the dry, parched cardboard homes along the railway line. Smoke quickly filled my room and I fainted through lack of air. I can't quite believe that I'm here, looking like this as surely my body would have been burned?"

Kaleem smiled back.

"My body is whole again too. It was smashed into trees as the wave pushed me along.
We can now begin to understand a little more about dying and being born again. I see none of my family nor the villagers but this is an enormous place and I'm sure they're here and as whole as me once more."

"My mother must be here somewhere too," she replied.

He looked around the room again as if to confirm that no one was recognisable. Perhaps he wasn't recognisable? Perhaps he had a different body now? He asked the girl about God.

"I am Hindu," she said. "Every day we used to give our seven offerings to the gods on a little Puja tray – fruits, seeds, wild flowers and rupees if we had any. On the tray there was a tiny bell that we would ring as we prayed and placed our gifts to our deities. Then my mother died. She was killed on the railway track that ran close to our homes. My father wouldn't let me see her. He cremated her in a field nearby. I am now beginning to hope that she would be made whole again like us. My father and brother were angry that my mother had been taken and they refused to pray. They felt our gods had let us down but I kept the tray and the bell and tried to place something – a leaf or a few rice seeds – on it every night before I went to sleep. I couldn't always find seven items to put there. These were meant to represent my senses to show my whole self was immersed in my worship. I tried my best so that I could ask God to care for my mother and to show that I still tried to love him."

"My God, Allah, meant more to me than anything," Kaleem confided. "I used to love being in the Mosque where I felt near to him. I feel we are close to him now and I believe that your god and my god are one in the same and that he loved us both and has been waiting for us since we were born. That's why we are here now in this queue about to find our place in a beautiful heaven."

He smiled, reaching out and touching her shoulder,

"It won't be long now.

"I know," she answered, nodding her head and touching his hand lightly.

Kaleem turned back towards the front.

When he had turned away, Aadhira thought about what he'd said. He was a muslim and she was a hindu. She had met people of other faiths before and never thought that they could all be one. There had been Christian volunteers at the first aid hut. They had come from religious organisations in England to help in the slums. Some of them were gentle and kind, thinking only of their patients and not of themselves. It was called missionary work but they had all told her that there was only one god and he belonged to them. They had said that if you didn't believe in their god and his son Jesus Christ, you would not be allowed to enter his heaven. Aadhira trusted the Hindu gods that her mother had told her about and she was puzzled by this. On one occasion, while waiting for some medicine for an infection, she had heard these christians discussing the accidents that happened daily on the railway line. In their conversation they had been agreeing that there were too many people in the slums anyway and the poor lives here were of little consequence. Aadhira had been shocked by this. What sort of god did they have who felt that some people were less important than them. Was it that their god was not good or was it the people themselves who were working in that god's name who felt this? Sometimes, she had been hurt by the reactions of the tourists on the railway station. Some grimaced and moved away when she had approached them. They looked down on her as if they didn't even regard her as a human being. They didn't know just how difficult it was and how dangerous to get across to the toilets on the other side of the track, nor did they know that it was hard to get water and that on many days, she was hungry because there was barely anything to eat. Why weren't they interested in the people who lived in the slums? She was part of real India but their interest was focused on the beautiful buildings, rarely the people, especially the poor ones. They chose not to remember that it was their politicians and soldiers that had taken India away from its people a long time ago. They'd used it for their own devices, treating the Indians as servants, removing their rights and their resources. When they handed back control, it was such a messy distribution of the land between the Muslims, Sikhs and Hindus that it led to fighting and killing and hundreds of thousands of people having to leave their villages and take their belongings to the opposite sides of the country. It created levels of poverty and distress from which the country was still recovering.

Now in the new India, these tourists seemed to look away, impatiently waiting to board their comfortable air-conditioned carriages in the train, ignoring their history. Aadhira realised that even her own people, of all faiths, also looked away. They never came near the slums as if leaving their smart houses and hotels in the new city would somehow taint them. They'd built a new city away from the poorest areas which were now left, deprived of money and of help. These affluent Indians did of course make money by sending tourists into the poorer areas in rickshaws pulled by boys so visitors could take home alarming photos of cows on the road, dogs lying dead in the gutters and people sleeping on the streets. They rode through the narrow lanes of the bazaars but never stopped to buy. Their purchases were from shops that had been specially set up for tourists.

One such rickshaw driver, for a short time, had been her brother. He had done it a few times when the need for money was greatest but he came home exhausted and broken with open sores on his bare feet and his shoulders bent from the strain. Her father had forbidden him to do it again. The tourists were told not to tip the "drivers" as they were paid by the tour companies but they didn't know how little they received for being used as animals.

She looked around now at the contrasting environment in which she had arrived. No more was she surrounded by frustration, filth, deprivation and squalor. In this beautiful place there was no anger, no suffering, no dirt, no shouting and no earthly needs to be met. She was clean and warm. She wasn't hungry or thirsty and seemed to have left behind all her emotions except a sense of peace and belonging.

Aadhira acknowledged that she had maintained her faith in her own small way despite her father and brother neglecting theirs and now it seemed she was here with this spiritual Muslim boy close to heaven.

Megan had arrived shortly after Aadhira. The terrible pain she had suffered had gone.

Now she stood in a line in a vast space which reminded her of the open expanses of land and sea around her islands. She thought about the wide sky, the wild sea and the machair that she'd left behind but there was no sorrow, just surprise and a growing excitement. She knew she was in a good place even though she had left her mother behind.

She was comforted by knowing that her mother had loved her deeply and she would be pleased to know that Megan was safe and whole again. She cast her eyes around the vastness before her. She saw the reflection of the glowing light coming from the entrance to which she appeared to be heading. The glow touched some of the figures who were silent and still. Like her, they wore white robes. She smiled as she thought how impractical these would have been had she been crossing the causeway from Benbecula and recalled again those stormy nights that had taken away her father's life and then her own. Here the air was as still as a calm summer's day. It offered her the space and confidence for her mind to accept what was to come. She knew it would be worth waiting for.

Megan's eyes returned to the queue. In front of her was a slight Indian girl who, at that moment, turned round and gave an assured and welcoming smile.
The girl had a pale, serene face which lit up when she saw Megan. Megan nodded to her, not knowing whether she could speak in this quiet place. Aadhira spoke first.

"We have travelled a long hard journey through life to arrive here," the girl suggested.

Megan nodded and could see that this simple girl was confirming her presence in the right place.

"Are we in heaven, do you think?" asked Megan.

Aadhira replied, "I'm sure we are close to God."

Megan looked abashed, "but I have not believed in god since my father was drowned in a storm. We used to go to the catholic church on my island every week, but we felt that god had let us down when we lost my father so perhaps God won't want me?"

Aadhira took Megan's hand in hers. Megan's hand seemed big in contrast to her tiny one.

"I think we've come near to god's presence and in my religion we are all part of god's family. I believe that this god is waiting for us all. Some of us have had to suffer on earth. Like your father, my mother died and I lived my whole life in a terrible slum where daily existence was almost a hell. What happened to you?"

Megan looked down at the girl's little trusting hand holding hers.

"I died because there was a fearful storm. I needed an operation but the wind made it impossible for me to be taken to a hospital where I could have received treatment and so survived. I can't believe that the pain has gone now. What happened to you?"

"There was a massive fire," said Aadhira, "and I was asleep when the flames reached me. There was nothing anyone could do. I look at myself now and I am amazed that I have my body back. I thought I'd become ashes. Maybe we have new bodies and we won't recognise those who had left us in our lives?"

Megan was beginning to understand.

"We don't need anyone now, only god. All our troubles are past and we have a wonderful life waiting for us. We don't even need to know what it will be like. I no longer have fear or anger or unhappiness. I will simply follow on after you."

Aadhira had never imagined that she would feel so confident and assured. She was glad to be surrounded by young people who were travelling in this new light with her.

Mark was the last to arrive. His voyage had been less straightforward. As he travelled, he had reached out to grab anything that could halt his advance into the unknown. It had been like a fairground ride, hanging on to a handrail while trying to reach the button that would make this journey stop. It was like his racing car dream all over again. Finally, his nightmare had come to an end and he found himself in a still, quiet place.

He stepped in angrily at first but then he found to his surprise that his anger was hard to hold on to. He looked around at his surroundings. Where was he? He must have died. All he remembered was the sound of a sports car driving fast along the seafront. He had turned just as the silver car hit him at high speed. He looked down at his body. It was intact without any apparent wounds. He was wearing a white robe like everyone else but there was not a sign of any blood or injuries. He didn't understand it.

Now he could see that he was at the back of a long queue which was almost stationary. He tried to look around the side of the queue and saw an opening from which a dazzling light shone. He tried to move to get a closer look and potentially jump the queue, but a strong force held him back and he was unable to move more than half a pace. Accidentally he knocked into the person in front. It was a young girl, about his age. She turned round and smiled at him quizzically.

"Are you all right," she asked him. He didn't smile back.

"Where are we?" he half snapped as he gazed at her perplexed expression.

"I think we are near to the presence of god," she said "and we are awaiting our turn to go through into the light."

Mark looked at her sceptically.

"It can't be to do with god," he retorted, "as I don't believe in all that stuff. I must have been killed in a car crash. I'm sure it wasn't my fault so I shouldn't be here at all."

Megan looked at him kindly.

"Don't worry," she said, "you are safe here and you will never have to suffer any discomfort ever again."

"I'm not sure I want to stay here," he answered, "this is not my sort of place although through that big hole in the wall where the light shines, it looks exciting."

"Oh yes," she said, "we are all going to be happy through there."

She nodded as if confirming to herself that she was as ready to move forward as the girl in front of her.

Mark turned and examined this large space more closely. Now he noticed there were other people, lots of them, maybe even hundreds of them, standing still in white robes like the one he was wearing. The space seemed to go on into infinity; no walls or ceiling to be seen, just fading into a distant haze. He watched these people. They were not in the queue, nor did they appear anxious to join. Although there were many of them, there was no sense of crowdedness, just a sense of peaceful waiting. These apparently dead people were mostly old. Their skin was translucent, their hair white. Their eyes were closed and their heads bowed. They looked comfortable; almost as if they had been asleep for a long time. Not a sound could be heard. There was nothing else in the space – no chairs, no tables with food and drink. Nothing, apart from this queue.

As he watched, the girl in front moved forward and he edged gingerly forward too.

What had she said about god? That couldn't be right. Or could it? Mark cast his mind back to his younger days at school when visiting women from the local church would come in to assemblies and tell stories from the Old Testament about Daniel who seemed to escape the lions' den and the fire because he believed in god. And about little David who killed the giant Goliath with a stone from his sling. He went on to become a king. Noah and his family were saved by the flood and two of every animal. There were countless stories that to be honest he had enjoyed listening to. When it came to readings from the New Testament, he had given them a mixed reception. The birth of Jesus was great because it led to the celebration of Christmas, acting in plays and all the lovely presents, holidays and food that that season entailed. He was not that happy about the visiting relatives who he found pretty boring but he was able to disappear after meals into his techie room to play with new games. They'd put a camp bed in there as the family members from afar needed his bed. It was great because they all had a lot to drink and didn't notice that he was up all night playing.

Mark tried to think of more stories. Jesus had been captured, tried and put on a cross to die and they said that this first Easter could celebrate new life with Jesus being born again. He didn't believe that nonsense anymore than he believed in the sugary niceness of those church folk delivering the stories. He'd heard rumours about their less than holy behaviour! Still, Easter meant mountains of chocolate eggs – so many in fact that often he was sick. He'd never been one to store up his treats. He wanted them all in one go, as in *now!*

His parents had often joked about miracles, especially the one they liked about turning water into wine. Jesus seemed to do a lot of bringing people back from the dead. However, in the bible, they woke up still in their own homes and villages. What about him? He hadn't woken up at home, had he?

The queue moved again – a few steps this time as he could see that several people near the front had gone through into the light space in quick succession. As he looked, he saw the man by the entrance tap the next person on the shoulder and direct him to a space in the room. Why was that, he wondered?

Mark began to think seriously about god and about behaviour. In his short life, he'd always had a laugh and didn't think he'd ever done any serious harm. Then he remembered the man Moses, right at the beginning of the stories. Moses had gone up into a mountain. There was something about a burning bush and seeing god with Moses returning with some rules. Now what were they called? There were ten of them. Ah yes, he remembered, the ten commandments.

Mark was a bit worried now. He tapped Megan on the shoulder and, as she turned towards him, he asked her for help.

"Can you remember the 10 commandments?" he asked her, "and can you explain what they mean?"

"Of course," she replied. "The first one is having no other gods."

"Well, that's easy then," laughed Mark, "I've never believed in any so that should be okay?"

Megan went on. "No, it means that you shouldn't love anything more than God."

Mark was silent realising he had loved his technology and his bike more than anything else.

"The second one," continued Megan, "is to have no idols. That means you shouldn't worship other human beings such as footballers, singers and TikTok stars by believing them to be better than others and following what they say and what they do."

Mark was silent again, so Megan carried on.

"Number three - taking the Lord's name in vain means not swearing using expressions such as 'oh god,' or 'Jesus Christ."

Taking his silence for understanding, Megan continued,

"The fourth one means keeping Sunday as a special day for god. I found this difficult after my father died as my mother and I stopped going to church every week."

"But hardly anyone goes to church now," argued Mark. "All the shops are open on Sundays and people are expected to work. That's not a reasonable rule so I shouldn't have been expected to keep that."

"What about honouring your mother and father?" Megan asked him. "That's an easy one, isn't it?"

Mark went quiet again, knowing that he had never respected his parents despite everything that they did for him. He saw them as facilitators of his every need. He had never even wished them happy birthday. Then he remembered that he had given his mother daffodils on Mothers' Day, even though he'd picked them from the roadside. Still he felt that might be enough.

"The sixth commandment is to not commit murder. I don't think we need to worry about that one," Megan smiled.

Mark thought about the birds' eggs he stole and the insects he tortured and dismissed them as not human. Meanwhile Megan was on to number seven, the one about committing adultery. Mark remembered laughing with his friends about this as it was something to do with sex and the word itself said "adult" so it was nothing to do with him. He had a passing thought that his shortened life had deprived him of experiencing love.

Megan was now on to number eight which was stealing. Immediately he lost his reassurance about the birds' eggs and there were several times when he had stolen money from his mother's purse. She knew of course but because she said nothing, he had assumed that it was a natural thing to do at his age and so it didn't matter. Then he remembered that he had stolen sweets and, occasionally, items from school – pens, pencils, even a compass as at the time he had thought it would be a useful tool with its sharp point. He had failed badly on this one.

Megan went on to remind him about number nine and not bearing false witness. This meant lying, not little white lies, but lies that could get someone into trouble. He'd done that lots of times, he realised.

Finally Megan came to the last commandment about coveting. He'd never really understood this.

"What does it mean?" he asked her.

"It means that you should be happy with everything you have in your life and, instead of being jealous about other people's possessions and achievements, you should be happy for them."

Well, this one came crashing down on Mark's head. He hated other children having things that he didn't have. He never wanted to say 'well done' to anyone. This was one of the worst and he was forced to acknowledge his behaviour.

Suddenly, Mark was realising what a horrible boy he'd been. Limply he tried to excuse himself and say it was his parents' fault for spoiling him but in truth he knew that they had tried to do their best for him. Why had he behaved like this? He had a comfortable, secure and loving home life. He was smart, athletic and confident.... and he had more than most of his peers.

Megan turned back as the queue moved forward.

Mark thought about the boy in his class at school who came every day in scruffy clothes and who never had money to buy anything from the sweet shop on the way home. Mark never thought to buy him some sweets or even give him some that he had stolen. What made him like this? If it wasn't his parents, then it was his personality. He was selfish and unkind, that was obvious but was that *his* fault. He'd been born like that surely. Anyone judging him in this place would know that, wouldn't they?

Mark kept thinking as the queue moved on. He watched people ahead of him moving through the gap into the bright light. No longer did he think that heaven might mean Christmas lights, endless fruit machines and fairground rides. He was beginning to understand what was truly important. He was shedding his inconsequential life for a more meaningful permanence. If only he could reassure his mum and dad. He looked at those standing away from the queue in the still, unmoving space. It dawned on him that

none of them were children. They were all adults and this gave him a growing sense of hope and expectation.

PART 3

Nothing beautiful can grow and flower

Where we have stood stubbornly

For years and years

Stamping on the earth

In our righteous boots.

Wake up!

Change.

Open your heart.

Love the world and help each other

And flowers will bloom again.

Our four young people were now near to the front of the queue with just a few ahead of them.
Each thought about their journey to this place.

Many of us dream of living on a small island in the Indian Ocean. In fact, lots of rich people pay large sums of money to share this isolated paradise for a few days. For Kaleem, this was home. He accepted its tranquillity and simplicity with a trust that told him he needed no more. In the azure seas surrounding his land, swim large green turtles flapping their delicate front 'wings" as they glide above the coral garden on the sea bed. Their bright eyes watching as they make their way through the lagoon. The huge Manta rays are alien spaceships with wide fins that carry them along like the albatross across the Southern Ocean. The shimmering reflection of the sun highlights the beautiful iridescent blue and yellow fish that weave peacefully among each other as the waving tree-like coral appears to reach out trying to touch. Kaleem remembered the day he heard a noisy colony of breeding sooty terns just inland from his favourite beach. He spent hours silently watching these slender, handsome brown and white birds as they prepared their nests to lay their one precious egg. Never did he dream of trying to hold an egg in his hand or take it for a rich supper. When the chicks had fledged, he had watched them fly off for their solitary life sailing above the oceans.

Kaleem recalled the majesty of the tiny mosque with its golden dome and the mystical words of the Imam. His fondest memory was saved for his special beach where he sat on the white sand alone among the gentle waving palm leaves and rippling waves. Most of all, he thought about his family. His tender mother who worked so hard along with his patient, strong father to give him everything he needed in life. He commemorated his grandfather, Nek Su, whose wisdom had fed his mind and soul with love and hope and compassion.

Now Kaleem was on the threshold of a new life for which he had been richly prepared.

Aadhira's mind went back to her impoverished upbringing. The slums of Delhi were a painful place to live. Lack of sanitation with overflowing toilets that were accessed by traversing the dangerous track and lying prostate beneath the trains as they sped past. Many people understandably wouldn't use the toilets which left the smells of excreta and urine in most parts of the slum. The water pump that was backbreaking to use and often only spurted out short bursts of dirty brown water. Without shoes, the walk to the forest was difficult and painful but it was worth it to harvest some of the fruits from the bushes. This had had its own dangers of course. A young girl on her own was easy pickings for the angry violent men who made this area their own and so her excursions to this mini paradise were limited to when she was with her mother and brother.

She had little comfort in her family shack right next to the railway line. All around her there was sickness and death. Lives here were of little value and in the scorching heat, bodies would be taken for cremation as quickly as possible and also struggling to keep alive meant there was little time to mourn those she'd loved and trusted. Aadhira was always thirsty as the dirty water was hard to come by. Her hunger was keen – her diet poor in nutritious elements. The fruits were either hard and unripe or mouldy as the birds were able to reach the branches and take their pick first. Rice, day after day, made a miserable diet but she was glad in the insecurity of her life to get any at all. She never complained as she knew that until she died on the track, her mother worked day and night to keep Aadhira and her brother from starvation and illness.

Aadhira felt that she didn't know her father at all. He was a shy man with not a lot to say. She only saw him briefly each day as he too laboured hard for the family. His simple acceptance had influenced Aadhira's mind so that she too was a meek and understanding girl. The rich tourists on the station platform seemed like another world to her and one, from occasional glimpses, of which she was glad not to be a part. There was a truth and honesty in poverty that could be corrupted easily by money and power.

Aadhira looked around the space she was in now and compared its white openness with the cramped and dirty room where she had slept and looked at the stars.

She was ready. In fact, she had always been ready.

This place sent Megan's mind back to the wide expanses of the Hebrides where , in the summer, she would cross the machair to find a small stream where she could dip her toes in the icy water. Golden eagles would fly across this open and wild terrain that was her home with the rugged mountains towering in the distance like guardians of the islands, the eagles their pilots of protection. She would gaze up in awe at these magnificent creatures with their mighty wings and then glance down as her toes were brushed by a darting, diminutive minnow, its stripes glimmering, reflecting the sun. The water sparkled and gurgled as if alive and she had wriggled her toes in delight. The breeze touched her face while she gently pinched the leathery leaves of a bright yellow primrose that grew on this lonely bank. She had bent down and scooped up some of the crystal clean water in her hands to drink.

Megan also recalled the raw winters when they all sheltered in the school house, huddled together by the cosy fire and learned about far off places like Africa and India where it was so hot and the seas were turquoise like those near these shores. The little ones listened in awe with Andrew trying to pretend that he wasn't interested while Mrs. MacKinley smiled and stoked the fire. The walks home had been exciting. On some days, the snow hurled itself horizontally at Megan with the stormy winds howling round and threatening to send her sliding across the icy path. On still days, when the sun occasionally shone, she was fascinated by the filigree lace patterns made by the ice and frost on leaves.

Home was warm and cosy too. She recalled her loving father who had adored her and carried her in his arms everywhere when she was little, making her giggle and squirm. After his drowning, she and her mother had formed such a tight bond. They were almost as one, both thinking of the other in everything that they did together; herding the diffident sheep, feeding the cantankerous, amusing hens and stroking the pink noses of the content cows whose dark, soft eyes stared back with tenderness.

This place, here now, was so different and yet so similar. Megan had felt the same spiritual bond as soon as she'd entered the vast room. This time there was no pain and she knew there never would be.

Now she was home again, just waiting for the final surge.

The transformation in Mark had been most remarkable. On entering the room, he had been ready to find fault and to accord blame to anyone or anything in his firing line. Merely, the atmosphere that he met had muted his frustrations into a questioning awe. He had spoken sharply to the girl in front of him in the queue but her kindness had fed into him like a calming medicine.

Mark thought back to his life in Great Yarmouth. He realised now that he'd been selfish. He'd made very few friends simply because he had always wanted, no – expected – his own way in everything. Now he looked back, he was amazed at how patient and kind his teachers and the other pupils had been in trying to befriend him.

Now Mark could see that all he'd ever wanted were possessions. He'd acquired them endlessly yet here there was nothing and it didn't matter! Those material things hadn't really made him happy. He could see that now. What had he missed while his focus was so wrong? He'd been to the undulating dunes where the tufts of grass had sheltered the larks' nests. He stole eggs where he should have been looking up in wonder at the lark singing high above with its melodious song. He could have walked along through the dunes and the soft sand to find the expanse of shore and the wide sky over the cold foamy waves of the North Sea.

Finally, Mark thought about his Mum and Dad. He had loved his father but perhaps for the wrong reasons. He had loved his Dad's emblems of success – cars, holidays, smart clothes his thriving business, all his socialising parties and his many friends. Mark admired all this but hadn't looked beyond to see how hard his father worked and the sacrifices he made to give Mark the best life as he could. It transpired that this hadn't really helped Mark, it had turned him into an obnoxious and selfish boy. He had despised his mother as she always fawned over him and gave in to his demands so easily. On reflection, he could see that she just loved him so much and that he had taken advantage of her. Perhaps it was the wrong sort of love. He was beginning to recognise that love must be open and free not claustrophobic and stifling.

Mark was amazed at just how far his thoughts had moved on. He looked at the man at the doorway with slight anxiety. He understood now and he hoped that the man would know that he had changed and he was ready.

They had all reached the front of the queue. Just one small group ahead of them;
two men, a woman and a child stepped through easily and disappeared from sight.

A further woman (looking a bit like one of Mark's old school storytellers), flushed with anticipation, was about to step in, but was held back gently by the man at the doorway. As he touched her shoulder, she turned and there was a surprised and uncompromising look on her face as though no one should question her right to go through. In her life, she had quietly taken her own path to its own ends, often displaying a loud confident laugh or giggly sense of fun to those she had chosen to be near. Here was someone who had followed her Christian religious duties to the letter with confidence but who had never put herself forward to consider anything from someone else's point of view. In fact, she didn't care. She knew what she wanted and she would get it with a quiet, yet blatant disregard for others. She was an adult, an older

adult in fact, so she had had years of opportunities to reflect on the effect her personality and actions had had on others.
Her blatant indifference had not always worked in her favour but she shrugged off these minor setbacks and came back renewed in indifference. She was not a child. Changing your personality is not easy but never reflecting or learning from the unhappiness caused to others is vital and it takes determination to make such a change.

Sometimes it was enough to be in this long queue for people to release their old habits and put on new, like Mark had done. A rebirth. Now, here in this place, this woman's over confidence in following her blind Christian doctrines had not given her the opportunity to reflect and change. She was not ready so now she would need more time in which to be reborn.

The man looked at her face which had become a mixture of anger and grief but he gently shook his head. With shoulders bowed and stubborn pride still mirrored in her face, she moved across to a space in the room where she would have all the time she needed to understand love and self-sacrifice.

Our four young people had watched this exchange. Kaleem and Aadhira understood. Megan felt confused although she had met some people like this in her church on Benbecula but she had thought *she* would be the unwelcome one because she didn't go to church.

Mark was very anxious. His eyes followed the woman's progress across the room until she stopped. Already there was a slight change of expression on her face. This was a place of hope from which no one would be excluded. For the first time, he noticed that there were no children in the space, although there were lots in the queue.

His hopes rose.

Kaleem stepped forward, turning to take Aadhira's hand and, without a backward glance, they flew into the light and were gone. Megan looked towards the man. He smiled at her and encouraged her to pass through and follow the others. Mark also turned. The man raised his hand and touched Mark on the top of his head. Then with his arm outstretched he gently eased Mark into the light where Megan, hand outstretched, beckoned.

"The beginning is always today" –

Mary Shelley

Printed in Great Britain
by Amazon

40448282R00076